The House Girl

UFUOMAEE

THE HOUSE GIRL

Copyright © 2018 Ufuomaee

All rights reserved.

ISBN: 9781983100215

This is a purely fictional work. Any resemblance to real persons, organizations or events is merely coincidental.

Photo credit: www.unsplash.com
Unless otherwise stated, all Scriptures referenced are from www.blueletterbible.org.

All rights reserved. No part of this book may be reproduced, stored in a retrieval system, transmitted in any form or by any means-electronic, mechanical, photocopying, recording, or otherwise-without prior permission in writing from the copyright holder.

DEDICATION

For all who hunger and thirst for righteousness and meaning through life's challenges.

AUTHOR REVIEWS

"You constantly allow God use you to correct the misinformation and vices in our world today and you do it in such a way that everyone gets the point. You really are amazing!"
- *Ifeoluwapo Alatishe* -

"Ufuomaee is a realist (I love the fact that she includes happenings in the society in her stories, sensitive topics we don't like to talk about. For instance, of sexual abuse in the Church and home as portrayed in The Church Girl and Broken respectively). Ufuomaee has that magical power to keep her readers spellbound. I also love the fact that she writes from a Christian perspective."
- *Jesutomilola Lasehinde* -

"Truly, you are one of the few people I delight in reading their posts. You make the book so real, I sometimes see myself as one of the characters. And I've been blessed by your books. You have a unique style of portraying your characters. You give them life."
- *Folashade Oguntoyinbo* -

"Ufuomaee is an author that writes fiction as though it is real. A Christian not ashamed to put her values into writing and I find myself reading the Bible passages she puts at the beginning of her stories. A great author whom everyone needs to read from."
- *Jimi Kate Darasimi* -

ACKNOWLEDGMENTS

I give God all the glory for this story. I had such an interesting experience writing it. I had many moments when the inspiration was flowing, and moments when I wondered at what a mess I was creating! But trust God to always to bring out the message in the mess. Because of this special experience writing The House Girl, I feel bolder about tackling more issues that concern our society and trusting God to shed His light.

Many thanks to my mother-in-law, Evelyn, who encouraged me as I wrote and was the first to listen to the first draft of the story. Your feedback was wonderful, as well as your help when it came to getting the broken English correct. Much love!

Thanks goes to Barr. Akinlami for sharing some of his legal knowledge with me as I constructed the story. Also, I really want to appreciate my friends and trustworthy reviewers, Chioma Oparadike and Ijeoma Awagu, for reading my manuscript and sharing their honest thoughts with me. Their feedback helped me to develop the story and bring more out of it.

I also want to thank my patrons at blog.ufuomaee.org and on Patreon for believing in me and encouraging me in this ministry. It means everything. You give me the confidence to keep writing, and of course, the push, so that I can entertain and inspire you with more stories. Thanks so much!

To everyone who buys and read my books, I'm truly grateful. Thanks for spreading the word, dropping your reviews and encouraging your friends and family to get their own copies too.

Finally, much love to my family, my rock, my home; Toju, Jason, Mom, Dad, Rhe, Kiwi, Jite and Ekechi. Thanks for always being there, inspiring and supporting me in your own special ways.

CHAPTER ONE

March, 2003. Garki District, Abuja.

"Chinyere! Chinyere!"

Madam's shrill voice sounded in the air, causing the house girl to raise her head slowly and rise up from her task of washing Madam's lace wrappers and beaded blouses, which she always demanded were hand-washed with her special soap. She rubbed her hands on her own cotton wrapper, which also substituted as a covering sheet at night, and wiped her hand across her sweaty face. The sun was particularly scorching today. She wondered what Madam could want now.

Pushing aside the mosquito net, and forcing the heavy steel kitchen door open, Chinyere walked into the kitchen to find Madam holding the pot of stew they had cooked yesterday. She had that look on her face that Chinyere was becoming accustomed to. That accusatory, demeaning look of privilege and superiority, not only economically, but spiritually. She steeled herself, ready for the accusations to flow.

"You are stealing meat from my pot again?!"

"Ma, I no steal..."

"Shut your mouth! Or do you think I am stupid?! You think I don't keep count of the meat in my pot? If it is not you, who broke into my house to steal meat?!"

Chinyere was quiet. No matter what she said, she knew she wouldn't be believed. Last time, when Madam had accused her, she had ended up begging and confessing to the theft, just so she wouldn't be thrown out. And now, she has been branded a thief!

"So, you will not answer today eh? Don't worry, you will see what I will do to you! You foolish girl!"

Chinyere stood there for a while, wondering if she should tell Madam that she hadn't been the one last time either. That she didn't like the constant false accusations. That she thought Madam was acting wickedly and delusional because she was miserable in her marriage. She didn't need to take out her frustration on other people. But she kept silent and watched as Madam went to the stove, muttering insults in her native tongue.

Chinyere returned to her washing under the hot sun, wondering what her punishment would be today. Her mates were at school, but for the past six months that she had been working with Mrs Peterson, she hadn't been privileged to attend, despite the promise made to her parents that she would. Her parents had been so happy to learn that Mr. Peterson was a rich, white man, and easily believed the promise that Chinyere would be sent to a good school in Abuja, where they lived.

Her Aunty Chinwe, who had gone to the village to persuade Mr. and Mrs Chukwuma to let their daughter follow her, had told her parents how the couple longed for a child of their own, and that Chinyere would be loved...not treated like a house girl. It sure didn't hurt that they got a large sum of money for agreeing to the arrangement. Even Chinyere had been excited about going to live in Abuja, in a rich white man's house. Even if she was a slave there, she was sure anything was better than remaining in her small village and trekking miles to school.

Of a truth, Mrs Peterson had been nice at the beginning. She'd been very chatty and friendly. Mr. Peterson was quite the opposite. A reserved man, who always spoke to her with formality, but respectfully. However, Mr. and Mrs Peterson were not happy, that much she knew.

Mrs Peterson forced herself on her husband constantly. She complained a lot about him not paying her any attention. The couple rarely spoke to each other and, when they did, it often led to arguments. Madam was anxious for a child, but it seemed Oga did not want to be bothered at all.

After a while, Madam had stopped trying to be nice to Chinyere. She was always irritable and suspicious. Chinyere knew she was miserable and prayed for her and her marriage. Even though it wasn't the best living environment, she needed the job, and she still believed that she would be enrolled in school for the next academic year.

***

Chinyere's rumbling stomach woke her up in the night. As she had expected, she'd gone to bed without dinner yesterday. All that had sustained her through the day was the bread and leftover scrambled egg she had eaten for breakfast. She sat up in bed and pulled at the curtain. It was nowhere near dawn. She still had about three or four hours of darkness and hunger until breakfast.

She decided she would go to the kitchen and see what she could nibble on. Even if it was just some groundnuts or a piece of bread. Madam usually wasted the crusts of the bread anyway. She wouldn't care, even if she noticed that it was missing, Chinyere thought or, rather, hoped.

She went first to ease herself, then crept in the dark to the kitchen. She was surprised to see a moving shadow and froze for a minute. She was actually more afraid to discover that it was her Madam than a Burglar. She blinked, and then the light over the small kitchen dining table came on.

Chinyere curtsied. "Oga."

"What are you doing up?" he asked.

"Sorry, Sir. I... I...de thirst." She couldn't admit that she was hungry, because he would think she was going to steal food. She picked up her cup, and filled it with water from the dispenser, before turning to leave.

"You're not hungry?" he asked.

Her stomach growled in response. "Small, Sir. But I dey fine until tomorrow."

"You can join me if you want..." he said, pushing a small plate of sandwiches across the table.

Chinyere looked at them like a hungry dog looked at a big piece of steak. She was so hungry it hurt. She nodded quickly and pulled out a stool to sit on. She took one small triangular shaped sandwich in her hand and it went in her mouth the same second. It tasted so good, she felt like she'd gone to heaven. She smiled, embarrassed. "Thank you, Sir."

"Why didn't you eat dinner?" Oga asked.

Chinyere didn't know how to answer him. She didn't want him to think badly of her, nor to be angry with her Madam. "I never hungry before... I dey do… Ummm…diet."

"You?" Oga looked at her in a way he had never looked at her before. In fact, no man had ever looked at her like that. She gulped. "You don't need to lose weight, dear. All you young people and your obsession with dieting."

Chinyere took another sandwich and said nothing. She wondered what Oga was doing up at this time, eating sandwiches in the kitchen. She'd noticed that he hadn't eaten much of his dinner last night. She wanted to ask him about it, but it was none of her business. She shouldn't repay his kindness with disrespect.

"How old are you?" Oga asked.

"Fourteen, Sir."

Mr. Peterson did a double take. The girl sitting before him

looked at least sixteen years old. Tall and full figured at 14 years, he marvelled. "Are you sure?"

His question was strange to her. Of course she was sure. "Yes, Sir."

"Aren't you supposed to be in school?"

Chinyere looked at him, confused. Didn't he know about her arrangement with Madam? "Madam say I don miss enrolment, so I go enter for next year."

"And miss a whole year of school?! No... You must resume next term."

"But I don already miss two terms, Sir. I go fail... And I go con repeat."

"Ummm... So, are you happy not going to school?"

"I dey read for house... Thank you, Sir." Chinyere swallowed her third sandwich and longed for the last one on the plate. However, she decided to leave it for Oga. "Good night, Sir."

He nodded at her, as she rose up from her seat to leave. He took the last piece of sandwich and watched her leave. She was just a child. All the while, his wife had told him she was sixteen years old.

She was the fourth house girl Osinachi had brought to stay with them, since they were married more than three years ago. They kept getting younger and younger. He had never put his mind to the matter of housekeeping before. But he liked Chinyere.

He drank some water and swallowed his medication, before arising to go back to his room.

***

"I want you out of this house this minute! You wicked, home-wrecking village girl!" Donald heard Osinachi shouting. That woman just didn't know how to keep her voice down. What was all this drama about this early morning?

Chinyere was crying. "I no do anything, Ma! Please... I no do anything wrong now..."

"You're a liar! You will pack your things and get out of my house now! Abi, you think say I be mumu! Idiot child!"

"What is all this commotion for, Osinachi?"

"This tramp is trying to steal everything that is mine in this house! She keeps lying, and I've had enough."

"What is missing?" Donald asked.

"Things... So many things... One day, it is meat. Another day, it is bread. Even the jollof rice I cooked for us, just the other day, didn't last two days!"

"Is that it? Food?"

"Eh... Well, I am even looking for my jewellery. And my wrappers that I gave her to wash are not complete. Please stop interrogating me. She has to go! I've had enough."

"If it is food that you are missing, then it's probably me. I also gave some of the rice to Ibrahim. The spice was too much for me, and I didn't want it to waste."

Osinachi looked at Donald as if he had just stabbed her in the gut. She turned on her heels and ran to her room, where she burst into tears. Donald hadn't wanted her to know that he couldn't stand her cooking lately. She was so sensitive about everything. But, it wasn't that he didn't like it. It's just that since he discontinued his old medication for a more common brand, he couldn't stand certain foods anymore.

Chinyere stood still before her Oga, waiting to know the verdict on her. Madam had been so cruel in her accusations. Why would she call her a home-wrecker? Did she think there was something between her and Oga? Maybe she had noticed them last night. Chinyere really wished she could clear up the misunderstanding, but there was no talking to Madam. She seemed determined to believe everyone was out to get her.

Donald looked at Chinyere. She looked shaken. "Please stay..." he said, apologetically. Chinyere nodded, and their eyes met briefly. In that instance, Chinyere saw that she was wanted. His eyes had communicated too much. And she suddenly felt guilty, as if it was true that she was indeed a home-wrecker, because she realised, in that same instance, that she wanted him too.

***

Later that morning, Madam came down from her room smiling. Oga had gone up to appease her, and Chinyere had heard Oga apologising. She was outside gathering the clothes, when she heard her Madam making those moaning sounds that she hadn't made in a while. She was happy that they had made up and hoped that things would be better for them. She silently prayed that Madam would have the child she longed for, so that the peace would last. She liked Madam whenever she was happy.

However, since that night in the kitchen with Oga, Chinyere had begun to see him in a different light. He had also become more verbal to her, and would ask her how she was doing, if she had eaten, and what she was reading, whenever he caught her resting for a while to read one of her academic books. He'd never shown any interest before. She liked the attention he gave her.

She also noticed that she behaved differently whenever he was around. She came out of her shell. She smiled a lot. She laughed, even when he didn't make a joke. She was conscious of her appearance, her movement and her speech, and hoped he would look at her the way he had done, very briefly, that night. But he did well to show her a fatherly love. So much so that she wondered if she had imagined the spark between them.

Oga and Madam made love frequently now. Chinyere was often kept awake with the sound of their lovemaking. It bothered her, whenever she imagined them in bed together. But at least, Madam was back to being nice to her, and even took to humming about the house.

Madam also hired a home-schooling teacher to take Chinyere on some classes, so that she would be ready to resume school in September. Chinyere knew in her heart that it was because of Oga, and love entered her heart for him. Overnight, her feelings for him changed from intrigue, respect and admiration to adoration, that she could barely keep out of her eyes.

CHAPTER TWO

Osinachi was happy. Things were finally looking up for her and her husband. After their first year of marriage, which had been wonderful as they were so in love, she had become stressed about their inability to conceive. Very quickly, her happy marriage became miserable, as she became obsessed with the idea of getting pregnant and subjected herself and her husband to various tests and treatments in her desire to conceive. However, nothing had worked.

But today, she'd missed her period. That ever reliable regular visitor was a few days late in coming, and Osinachi was beaming. She knew she was pregnant. She just knew it!

She didn't want to take a pregnancy test. She just wanted to see her doctor. She was sure he would confirm that she was pregnant and advise her on what to do next. She felt so different in her body; her breasts were tender in a way that they'd never been before, and her abdomen felt constricted. Although she didn't feel nauseous nor have other common signs of pregnancy, she was sure that her prayers had finally been answered.

"Hmmm..." Doctor Uly muttered as he studied the printed results before him. He looked up at Osinachi and tried to smile. "Well, I can confirm that you are indeed pregnant..."

"Yes! Jesus! Yes!" Osinachi jubilated and tried to sit still. She was so excited, she didn't notice the frown on her doctor's face, as he waited for her to calm down and let him finish. "Okay... I'm so glad I've been taking my multivitamins. Is there anything else you recommend, Doctor?"

"This is your first pregnancy, right?"

Osinachi nodded, excitedly. "Yes, it is."

"Yeah... Considering the delay you've had, I would like to be able to rule out anything that may mean that this pregnancy will be problematic. But, I'm afraid that I can't give you any such assurance."

"What do you mean, Doctor?" Osinachi asked, leaning forward and frowning.

"Well, your β-HCG level is rather high... It is possible that you might have an ectopic pregnancy," he swallowed.

Osinachi swallowed too. She'd read about those. But she wanted him to tell her what exactly the problem was. "I don't understand."

"The existence of β-HCG, a special hormone secreted by the developing embryo and placenta, is a sure sign of pregnancy. However, high levels of it is usually an indicator for ectopic pregnancies. These are pregnancies outside of the uterus, where the embryo has been implanted in one of the fallopian tubes."

Osinachi swallowed. "But, it may just be normal, right?"

"Yes... It may. But we need to do more tests to be sure. If you do have an ectopic pregnancy, I'm afraid the fetus would have to be aborted as soon as possible, as this pregnancy would become life threatening to you."

Osinachi had stopped listening when the doctor mentioned abortion. She couldn't believe it. She didn't want to believe it. She would pray. *God, you can't take my baby away!* Silent tears rolled down her cheeks, and Osinachi was brought back to the present with the movement of the box of tissues on the doctor's desk in her direction. She took one and dabbed her eyes and cheeks.

"I'll schedule you in for a transvaginal ultrasound this Friday. Hopefully, that should rule out any ectopic pregnancy. Don't worry, Osinachi. Keep praying. Miracles happen every day," Doctor Uly said to console his patient, even though he wasn't really all that optimistic.

***

Osinachi decided to go to the Church to see her pastor, after the doctor's visit. She needed her counsel and her support in prayer. Pastor Tosin Omole had prophesied over Osinachi every year for the last three years that she would have a baby that same year. She'd even said she'd had dreams about it and said that all Osinachi needed to do was to believe enough, and to add to her prayers charity and good works. This Osinachi did by giving generously to her Church and becoming more active in the Fellowship.

"This is it, Osinachi! God has done it for you already. Don't let the enemy take the seed of promise from your heart! Have faith in God and don't doubt. You will carry your baby in nine months!" Pastor Omole said, when Osinachi had told her of her pregnancy and the doctor's report.

"Whose report shall you listen to?! Men or God's? God has said it, and I know that you should have conceived since, but your faith is not strong enough. Also, there may be sins in your life that is hindering your blessing. I will pray for you, my daughter."

"Thank you, mommy," Osinachi said, thinking that Pastor Omole was so in the spirit and discerning. Obviously, her faith hadn't been strong enough. She wouldn't doubt but believe that it is already done in the supernatural and will soon manifest.

"The Lord is asking you to sow a seed... A seed

proportionate to the blessing you desire. Between now and Friday, sow your seed in faith, and you will not be disappointed, thus says the Lord!"

Osinachi nodded, thinking she would double her tithe this month. She would pay the full tithe now in faith and pay again at the end of the month. By then, she'd be assured that her pregnancy is normal and healthy. She'd been sowing seeds for years, but she couldn't doubt God. She couldn't doubt her pastor. God knows that she'd do anything, apart from give her body to be burned, to have a child.

As she left her pastor's office, Osinachi took a call from her sister, Daluchi. They hadn't spoken in a couple of weeks. But Osinachi wasn't sure if she was ready to disclose her news to her.

"Hey, Dal," she answered.

"Hi, dear. How are you?"

"I'm fine oh. What's up?"

"It's about the girl I told you about the other time. When are you going to come and see her?"

"Ummm… I'm really not chanced right now. I hope there's no problem."

"No problem, oh. Just wanting to make sure you're still interested."

"Sure. I'll send you some more money. I'm sorry, I'm a little distracted right now."

"Okay. Thanks. We'll talk later."

After Osinachi dropped the call, she wondered why she hadn't been able to proclaim in faith that she was an expectant mother. But Daluchi was helping her with an important favour, that she didn't want to compromise until she was certain of her hope. And for now, she wasn't. *Lord, please help my unbelief*, she prayed.

***

It had been over a month since he started noticing his house help, Chinyere. The girl was not fair to look upon, and so he hadn't paid much attention to her before. He was often drawn to light-skinned women, like Osinachi, who had pronounced features. Chinyere was a different sort of beautiful. It took a special eye to see and appreciate her beauty. She was the kind of girl that a model scout would approach for a contract. A unique look, not classically beautiful but aesthetically pleasing. She would definitely grow into a knock-out.

The glass partition between his study and the living area allowed him to study her discretely, as she took her lessons for the day. Before, she'd started, he'd had her bring him a cup of tea, while he read his newspaper. He'd been surprised to see that she'd brought it with ham and cheese sandwiches. He'd liked that special touch; the fact that he didn't request for them and she'd taken the initiative, and the fact that she knew what he liked. She liked him. He was sure of it. But what did it mean?

Donald took a sip of his tea and relaxed on the armchair. He always enjoyed these early morning times in his office, which now coincided with Chinyere's Saturday lessons. Osinachi often slept in or had one Church meeting or the other to attend. Today, she'd slept in.

He'd noticed there was something off about her yesterday. He'd asked her about it, and she'd just complained of a headache. Well, it was becoming typical Osinachi, even though he thought she'd finally laid to rest her anxieties about getting pregnant. Things had been better between them over the last month, sexually. He'd sought her out more often, because he was feeling a lot more randy these days. And he knew the reason why.

He wanted Chinyere. He'd had to admit that to himself some weeks back, after he'd made love to Osinachi, but was still feeling in need of something else. He'd seen Chinyere minutes after and he knew. She was the something else.

He sighed deeply as he contemplated his predicament. She

was just a child. It was such an unusual and dangerous attraction. But that itself made it exciting. He often played around with ideas of how he could satisfy his craving without anyone finding out about it. If Chinyere liked him, like he thought she did, surely, such could be arranged. If only just once. And then his curiosity and need would be satisfied. He might even let go of her after that, just so it doesn't become a full-blown affair.

He swallowed. *This is crazy! You cannot seriously be thinking of cheating on Osinachi with her house help,* he scalded himself! *And remember, she's just a child!*

Chinyere's lesson had concluded, and her lesson teacher had risen to make his exit. Donald watched as she got up to escort him to the front door and locked it behind him. She made her way back to the dining area to gather her books and study materials, which she then took to her room. Some moments later, there was a knock on the door to his study.

"Come in," Donald said, looking up to see who it was, though it could only be one of two people.

He was happy when he saw that it was Chinyere. She walked towards him, and he was transfixed as she bent down to carry the tray on the coffee table to take to the kitchen. "You like?" she asked, shyly.

He gulped. His manhood had instantly responded to her presence and the two simple words she'd spoken, so enchantingly. "Yes," he breathed. "Very much". And when she smiled, he knew that she knew that he was hot for her. *If only she was a couple years older... If only.*

***

It had happened before. Though, that time, it wasn't really his fault. Well, not totally. She'd come after him. And unlike the others, she wouldn't take "No" for an answer.

Being a rich, handsome, white man, it wasn't strange for many African women and girls to throw themselves at him. He was in high demand, and Osinachi knew that even before they had gotten serious. She'd fought a few off in the months before their wedding. And to his credit, he had been faithful.

But this young fox, Gbemi, had been determined. And strategic. She had been his secretary. Well, a temp that became his secretary.

It had happened in the second year of their marriage, when Osinachi was depressed about not having a baby, and he was tired of her going on and on about it. He'd decided to stay later at the office, and Gbemi had stayed to assist or keep him company. She'd made her move, and well, he'd been unable to resist.

Well, that ultimately imploded on itself. Gbemi was too crazy and greedy for her own good. After a couple of months, she was seeking a promotion AND a relationship. She thought they were in love… She threatened to tell his wife. She even threatened to report him for sexual harassment when he denied her the promotion. He had been forced to tell Osinachi.

And to her credit, she'd been his strength. She'd forgiven him and fought off Gbemi, whose reputation for seducing and manipulating executives was well known. The leach was removed, and he'd promised never to betray his wife's trust again. But did he really have what it takes to be a faithful husband? He was soon to find out.

CHAPTER THREE

Chinyere was singing as she scrubbed the bathroom tub. She was so happy because, earlier that week, her lesson teacher had informed her that she'd passed the mock exams he had given her the previous week, and she would be able to enter direct to SS1 with the next set of students. At a few days shy of fifteen years old, she was already late starting, but he had assured her that there was no race nor hurry, and that because she was bright, if she kept up her studies, she would surely excel in all her exams.

She remembered how thrilled Oga had been when she had shown him her results yesterday. He'd looked at her with such intensity in his eyes, that her stomach had tightened in response. But all he'd said was "Yeah! Well done, Chinyere! I knew you could do it." She'd released all her emotion in a wide smile, as her heart swelled with heat. Her eyes were shining as she'd responded, "Thank you, Sir." Madam had only said "Congratulations!" and added "Money no waste" cheekily.

This weekend, she would be going home to her family for her leave. It was only the third one she was taking since she began working for the Petersons nine months ago. She was eager to show them her results, knowing they would be so happy and proud to learn that she was doing well. It was also her birthday weekend, so she was keen to have it off.

Madam was on the phone, and she was promising someone that she would be in Lagos tonight or tomorrow morning unfailingly. Chinyere's ears itched as she heard her, hoping that her planned leave would not be affected. She finished with the bathroom, and Madam quickly entered it and locked the door. An hour later, when Madam was dressed and packed ready to leave, Chinyere thought to confirm her leave for this weekend.

"Ma," she started nervously. "It is my off tomorrow."

"Oh," Madam muttered. "When did we agree that?"

"Last month, Ma. I tell you. You say e dey fine, I fit go."

"I don't remember that. But, you can go next week... I have to travel urgently, and I need you to attend to a few things at home. I hope you don't mind..." She said this, as she made her way to the door.

"Ma... Please, I no fit stay. I really want my off!"

Osinachi stopped, turned and looked at the girl. Why was she being so demanding and rude? This was about control and respect, and lately, the girl had been seeking every opportunity to assert herself. Her friends had told her that it is because she's too nice to her, that's why she had the mouth and gall to talk back. Osinachi eyed her, annoyed.

"I have told you you can have next weekend! Please stop wasting my time and carry this bag out to the car!!"

***

Osinachi had called Donald to let him know about her urgent travel plans. She said she might be back tomorrow or the day after. So, he knew that he would be home alone tonight with Chinyere. The thought filled him with anticipation and anxiety.

Over the past couple of months, she'd dominated his thoughts. They didn't say much to each other, but their eyes communicated so much understanding of an attraction that he was sure was mutual. But even if he could get over the fact that she was his house girl, he couldn't get over the fact that she was still a child... He was almost three times her age for goodness sake!

Donald let himself into the house with his keys and found the dining table set for one. Chinyere came out of her room and immediately curtsied. She was avoiding his eyes.

"Welcome, Sir," she said, and went to collect his briefcase from where he had placed it by the sofa.

"Thanks, Chinyere. Dinner smells good. How was your day?"

She looked up and smiled briefly, giving him a very momentary eye contact. "It was fine, Sir." She didn't ask about his day. He noticed. She was definitely uncomfortable with this arrangement. He watched her as she took his things up the stairs to his room.

When she came back down, she headed straight for her room, though he'd hoped she would linger in the living room and he could invite her to join him. He sighed and decided it was best that way. He served his dinner and ate alone while he watched the news.

Chinyere came out about an hour later and cleared up the table. Oga had retired to his room, and she'd heard the shower running. She quietly did the dishes and tidied up the kitchen. She was surprised that there seemed nothing else to do, and it wasn't even 9pm yet. Whenever Madam was around, there seemed always something to do. Or was it just that she felt she had to keep busy whenever her Madam was around, or because Madam always had something for her to do, right up to bedtime?

"I thought it was your weekend off..." she heard Oga say from the doorway. Her heart raced, and she turned around to face him. He was wearing his dark blue, cotton shorts and a white t-shirt, revealing broad shoulders and hairy, muscular, fair limbs. He was so handsome!

"Yes, Sir." She was pleased that he had remembered.

"So, why didn't you go? I would have been fine on my own..."

"Madam say make I take next weekend off."

"Okay... Good. You okay?" Donald couldn't help but ask. There was something sad about her countenance tonight. He had expected her to be...different. Happy, maybe.

Chinyere nodded. "Yes..." but a tear rolled out of her eye. She quickly wiped it and turned around towards the sink again. "I am fine, Sir. Good night."

Donald was positive she was crying, but he couldn't understand why she would. He hoped she was not afraid of him. He swallowed. "Have you eaten?" he decided to ask instead.

She nodded vigorously.

"Okay..." He retreated into the living room to settle on the sofa. He wished she would tell him what the matter was. Had Osinachi said some nasty things to her again? He decided not to worry about that either. She was not his friend. She was his house help. So, why was it at the tip of his tongue to ask her to join him to watch his TV show?

Chinyere went back into her room without saying another word. She was behaving quite oddly, Donald thought. She was not this shy when Osinachi was around. *Maybe because nothing could ever happen with Osinachi around...* Now, all that restrained them from doing what they both desired to do was self-will and self-control. And that thing called conscience.

He heard her shower running and struggled to keep the thought of her washing naked out of his mind. He wasn't paying any attention to his show. Who was he kidding? He switched it off and brought out the newspaper he had been reading in the morning. He was still reading the same page 15 minutes later, as he kept re-reading lines and paragraphs.

Frustrated with the tension he was feeling, he grabbed his keys, slipped his feet into a pair of slippers and went for a long drive.

***

Chinyere was still awake when she heard Oga open, shut and lock the front door, upon his return. Her glow in the dark wristwatch told her that it was five past one in the morning. She turned in her bed.

She wished he would knock on her door and check in on her. She wished she had not been so emotional earlier and had watched TV with him, as she sometimes did when Madam was around. She wished she was bolder to go to him, without fear of his rejection. She wished she didn't feel this way. She didn't want to be a home-wrecker.

She heard him in the hallway. For a while, she heard nothing. She held her breath, wondering if he was going to open her door. Then she heard his footsteps on the stairs, and knew he was going up to his room. Disappointment filled her heart, and she cried. She was a bad girl for having such thoughts...such hopes.

***

Donald plumbed on his bed in a drunken state. The alcohol in his bloodstream made his limbs and eye lids heavy, so that sleep came easily to him. It was the only way to stop the recurring thoughts he had about taking Chinyere. He had to do anything else but that this weekend. And drinking was easy to do.

Of course, he had hoped that his drinking would affect his judgment significantly, so that he would be able to come home and do what he longed to do, without his conscience getting in the way. Then he could blame it on his drunkenness. But as he'd stood outside Chinyere's door tonight, he'd realised that he was still capable of cognitive thinking. And besides, the way he was feeling towards her, he wanted to be sober when he took her. He wanted to remember everything about it.

Why did Osinachi leave him alone with this temptation?

She should just hurry up and come home, he thought as he drifted off to sleep.

***

"Good morning, Sir," Chinyere greeted.

Today, she looked radiant and was bolder about greeting him. What happened to the sad, shy girl from last night, Donald wondered? And was she dressed up...with make-up?! *Oh crap!*

"Good morning, Chinyere," he replied, taking his seat at the dining table. "Did you sleep well?"

"Yes, Sir," she smiled happily, as if she had a secret.

"Hmmm... This is lovely. Are you going to join me?" Donald asked before he could think. Then, he was pleased he did. She nodded happily and pulled a mat out for herself and began to serve a plate.

Donald swallowed when she sat next to him. She smelt like a rose garden, so sweet. He looked at her and dared to hold her gaze. She blushed. "You are looking different today..."

Chinyere giggled. "Do you like it?" She'd spent at least 30 minutes on her make-up today, using the cosmetics Osinachi had discarded a few months ago. She knew they would come in handy one day.

He breathed in deeply. This was the Chinyere he had hoped to come home to last night. Why was she so different this morning? He looked at her again, and openly admired her. "Yes, it's nice. But, are you going somewhere?"

Chinyere shook her head. "No... It's my birthday..." she almost whispered.

Donald's eyes glowed as he looked at her. *Wow...* So, she was now fifteen... "Oh, wow. I didn't know. Happy Birthday!" She beamed. "Is that why you wanted to take the weekend off?" She nodded shyly. "And why you were sad yesterday?"

"You notice?" she asked, gently. She still wasn't good with

her tenses, though her English was improving, and she was enjoying learning and practicing new words.

"It was hard not to. You were not yourself."

"I'm sorry, Sir. I hope I no offend you."

"No... It was fine." Donald swallowed. This was news... He wasn't sure what he was going to do with it, but he liked her mood...and her dressing...and her boldness. His stomach tightened. "So, what do you want to do today?"

"I want to watch TV with you..." she said that so simply, that it felt romantic. Donald couldn't look her in her eyes. He was too happy to hear her say that. He was too afraid of what it meant for his chances of keeping her at arm's length today. "If you want..."

Donald realised she had expected a response from him. He gathered his emotions and looked at her, trying to give her that fatherly smile he sometimes gave her, but he was too mesmerised by her beauty today to pull it off. He coughed nervously. "That would be nice."

They exchanged a look of understanding. Today, there would be no fronting. They were going to relax, enjoy each other's company and just do what comes naturally...

Breakfast happened without incident. They enjoyed an electric silence between themselves, with the sound of the TV like a distant background noise. After breakfast, Chinyere cleared up and washed the dishes, while Donald went to his room to get some condoms before returning to lounge on the sofa. He sat waiting in both anticipation and trepidation. He wished he could be bold enough to tell her to forget about the dishes and come and sit with him. But he also wanted to be cool.

When she returned, she sat awkwardly beside him, and he giggled thinking this was the same bold girl who had said she wanted to watch TV with him for her birthday. He made the first advance as he slid his hand on her thigh. He closed his eyes as he did that, afraid that she would push it away and tell him he had the wrong idea. But she didn't.

He then slid his hand over her shoulder and pulled her closer to him. She looked up at him, and in the next second, their lips met in a soft kiss. They smiled at each other, but it was only brief, as Donald pressed his lips against hers eagerly and ran his free hand along her body, lingering to caress her breasts.

The TV no longer mattered. It was just them, and their passion. Donald half-willed his conscience to kick in, but he knew that had been thoroughly subdued already. The burning in his loins couldn't wait, not when Chinyere was touching him the way she was.

He grabbed her roughly and pulled her to lay beneath him. They undressed each other eagerly, kissing desperately. He savoured every scent, taste, feel and sound in their foreplay, before he took her on his sofa. And yes, he would remember every touch, stroke and movement of their sexual intercourse.

CHAPTER FOUR

It had been a long night for Osinachi. She'd arrived in Lagos around 8pm and had headed straight to the hospital. Her sister had given her the details for the room they had booked, and she was shown the way at the lobby to the Maternity Ward.

Daluchi met her in the hallway and told her that everything was going according to plan. The girl was doing fine, but she wasn't well dilated yet. She assured her that at the rate things were progressing, Osinachi could be home with her "special gift" as soon as next week.

Osinachi had only met the girl once. Today, she was looking healthier, having gained much weight due to her pregnancy, and being well looked after by Daluchi. Osinachi watched as the girl grimaced, squeezing her eyes shut and sucking in a harsh breath, as she rode through another round of contractions. She felt both happy and sad watching the girl in labour. Sad because she'd had to abort her own baby, and happy because she was not the one going through that pain of child birth and would soon be embracing her first child.

Baby Benjamin was born at 3:45am that Saturday morning. He was a beautiful child at 7.6lbs, with a full head of matted black curls, and big dark eyes. Osinachi loved him the moment she saw him and was overjoyed when she finally got to hold him in her arms. The mother had shown no interest in carrying the boy, only to take one look at him. Her son was almost a carbon copy in likeness.

Osinachi was pleased and relieved with how easily the transaction had been completed. She'd signed the legal documents Daluchi had prepared with the help of a Lawyer, and they had been able to take the baby boy home with them that evening. Osinachi had previously considered returning home and coming back next week to take Benjamin home, but after seeing him and carrying him, she knew she didn't want to leave him for a second. She rescheduled her return trip for Tuesday morning, after confirming with the airline that she could carry the newborn onboard.

Despite her excitement at finally having a baby, Osinachi was distraught. She remembered when she had first told her elder sister of her desire to have a baby via a surrogate. She'd expected her to shut her down and tell her that she was being impatient and distrusting. But Daluchi had been very practical and said that it was something she could help her with. In her profession as a Nurse at the General Hospital, she knew of many women and girls who wanted to abort their babies, and she had managed to divert some to consider adoption instead. It all seemed so simple.

Osinachi had discussed the idea of adoption with Donald back then, but he hadn't been keen. He'd said that she was worrying needlessly and was sure that they would eventually get pregnant, if she would stop stressing over it. They'd done the needful tests, and they were both healthy. Apart from some fibroids that Osinachi had to have removed, nothing appeared to be hindering their ability to conceive. So, Osinachi had let it go and decided to pray harder. It was then she began to give tithes faithfully at Church, just in case her inconsistency in this regard had closed her womb.

Then three months ago, Daluchi had called her about a young lady, Uloma, who had been attending the Ward with her boyfriend, but who recently expressed suicidal ideation. After taking the lady aside to talk to her, and find out what the matter was, the girl told her how the father of the child had abandoned her and would be marrying someone else, who was also carrying his baby! She didn't want to continue with her pregnancy, but she was too far gone to abort it. Daluchi wanted to know if Osinachi would have the baby.

It really wasn't the way Osinachi would have wanted it to happen. Ideally, she would have wanted a gestational surrogate, someone who would carry her egg, fertilized by Donald's sperm if he had agreed. At least, she would have loved to have known about the pregnancy earlier on, and learnt more about the mother and father, whose genes her adopted child would inherit. However, the other cases Daluchi had brought to her were as a result of rape, prostitution, and even one-night stands, where the mother didn't even know the father.

This case was different, and it seemed special. She'd reasoned, "*God works in mysterious ways*", and decided to accept this special gift. Daluchi had followed up with the girl, and even accommodated her for the remainder of her pregnancy. The poor girl had run away with her boyfriend to Lagos, after he had impregnated her and her parents had rejected his proposal to marry her. She had been too afraid and ashamed to contact her family and confess what had happened to her.

What troubled Osinachi now was that they had not yet been able to get a hold of the father of the child to confirm the girl's story, and also sign off his paternal rights to the child. Osinachi also worried about how Donald would feel about the baby. Up till now, she hadn't been bold enough to tell him. As things had improved between them, and they were frequently intimate sexually, she'd hoped that she would conceive before Uloma put to birth. And as the time neared the delivery date, it had become harder and harder to bring up the child to Donald.

Ideally, she should have told him when she lost her pregnancy almost two months ago. But she'd been too depressed about it. She was also struggling with her faith in God. She was determined to have this child. She didn't want to risk losing it by having Donald say "No". She knew that in time, he would understand why she had to do it.

Osinachi looked down at Benjamin sleeping in his crib as they rode home from the hospital. She never knew she could love another unrelated human being so much, over such a short time. She was bound to this child. She could never put him up for adoption or leave him in another's care. He was truly hers... Her one and only son.

***

Osinachi decided to return with Benjamin on a weekday morning, knowing that Donald would be at work. It would give her time to prepare how to introduce him to his new son and prepare his favourite meal and a seductive treat as well. Being a business woman, who travelled often, Donald had not been suspicious about her recent get away, nor of her call on Sunday, when she had said she had some meetings to attend on Monday and would be leaving for Abuja afterwards, or at the latest, Tuesday morning.

Osinachi arrived at the house at about 11am and was warmly received by Chinyere. The girl's shock came moments after, when she saw the stroller, and heard the little baby's cry. Chinyere quickly assisted her madam with her bags, noting the protective way Osinachi clutched the stroller.

"Welcome, Ma."

"How are you?" Osinachi asked, without showing any interest in the answer.

"Fine, ma," Chinyere duly replied. She wanted to ask about the baby but didn't know how. She lingered around her madam, hoping for an opportunity to look more closely at the infant. Eventually, she asked, "Can I help with Baby, Ma?"

"No. Not yet. Take my things upstairs and clean out Baby's room."

"Baby's room?" Chinyere was shocked. She hadn't noticed any baby things in the house since she had been living there. How secretive was Madam?

"Yes! The one that is locked upstairs. You'll find the key in my top drawer. Hurry up!"

Osinachi watched as Chinyere hastened to her task. She probably shouldn't have told her where she kept the key. But she was sure there was nothing else private in her top drawer. Only some medicines she kept.

She sighed and petted her little darling. Time to make him feel right at home. Now, how was she going to break the news to Donald...?

***

It had been an incredible long weekend, filled with heightened emotions and illicit sex. Donald had indulged himself to his heart's content, surprising himself at the extent he went to satisfy his grave passions, without shame. Chinyere was easy to teach and lead in bed. She had also been eager to please. They had exhausted themselves on the first day, and he had felt only momentary anxiety and dread that Osinachi would be returning that Saturday.

By Sunday morning, the guilt had kicked in. They'd slept in separate beds, not wanting to be found in each other's arms in the morning if and when Osinachi returned. Donald slept in late, and when Chinyere knocked to inform him that she'd made breakfast, he'd turned it down.

Donald had tried to keep Chinyere at arm's length on Sunday, as he'd been convinced that his wife would be returning that day from her travels. He wanted to get himself together, and his mind on something other than his maid. When he'd finally gotten up and bathed, he'd spent the rest of the morning in his room and caught up on some reading. It was not good for business nor for his life to have an affair with someone who lived right under his nose. *What was he thinking?*

Osinachi could be hard to live with, but he knew he still loved her. He'd remembered how they had met and fallen in love, and his promise to be faithful and loyal the rest of their days together. Okay, so he'd messed up before, but it wasn't something he planned on making a habit. And Chinyere was the worst kind! She was their maid...and a child and a definite no, no! What had gotten into him?

He'd eventually left his room at lunchtime, hungry for food. He'd gone to the kitchen and found rice, stew and fried plantain already made. He'd smiled, thinking how efficient Chinyere was. He'd served his plate and sat at the dining table to eat. He'd half-expected her to come out of her room and join him, and half-hoped she wouldn't.

Chinyere had spent the rest of the afternoon in her room. He'd suspected that she was probably upset with him for ignoring her. All the same, Donald decided to leave the house to avoid any temptation. He met up with a few of his friends at the Bar and Lounge he frequented on Sundays. He intended to stay away until Osinachi called to say she was back.

However, at about 6pm, she'd called to say that she had to stay back for some meetings and wouldn't be returning until Monday evening. Donald was not prepared for the elation and excitement he'd felt at her announcement. He'd not been able to pay attention to the match on TV, nor join the banter with his friends after that.

He'd returned to a quiet and clean house at 7pm. His dinner had been set, but he wasn't interested in that. He'd headed straight for Chinyere's room and knocked. He knocked again when the response he'd expected didn't come.

Eventually, Chinyere had opened the door for him. She'd

looked downcast, as she avoided his eyes. "I hope no problem, Sir?"

That'd been it. He'd taken her in his arms then. *Age ain't nothing but a number...* The popular Aaliyah track played in his mind. This was consensual, he'd told himself as he stripped her of her night clothes and had sex with her on her bed.

And the next night, when Osinachi still hadn't returned, the indulgence continued.

Today was the moment of truth. Donald was returning home to face two ladies he was intimate with. Sure, one could hardly be called a lady, but she was a young lady nonetheless. He didn't know how long he could keep this up, or even if he would be returning home to trouble. So, he'd decided to come home armed.

***

Osinachi opened the door to her husband, dressed in a sexy, pink lace lingerie set she hadn't worn in a long time. She was pleased to see the excitement and pleasure in his eyes as he appraised her. If he was surprised, he didn't show it. But she was definitely surprised to see that he had also bought her flowers and chocolates. He hadn't done something so romantic since Valentine's day. What was the special treat for?

Osinachi took the gifts from him shyly. She smelt the bouquet of assorted flowers. "This is lovely, Donald. Thank you." She was curious about the meaning of the gesture, but she was more aware of the meaning of her gesture, and what she was hoping to achieve tonight. There was no way his secret could top hers. "It seems we had the same mind tonight," she said flirtatiously, instead.

Donald took his wife in his arms, smiling wildly. This was way better than any way he had imagined tonight turning out. Was that chicken and mushroom pie he could smell? He sniffed happily, about to comment on the meal his wife had prepared for him. Was that a baby crying? He frowned and looked into his wife's eyes, when he was sure of the sound. There was a baby in his house...

Osinachi swallowed. "Darling, we need to talk."

CHAPTER FIVE

"Osinachi, what's the matter with you?!"

"Donald, I did it for us!"

"NO! No! You did *this* for yourself! How could you plan this without me?"

"It wasn't like that, Baby..."

"Don't! Don't Baby me... I don't even know who you are anymore. God! All these secrets and lies...!"

"Please, Donald... Please! I'm begging you. Just give him a chance..."

"You talk as though I have a choice. I can't believe this... I'm... I need some fresh air!"

"Donald!"

Moments later, Chinyere heard the front door slam shut and Madam breakdown in sobs. Why did Madam do such a wicked thing? Chinyere looked down at the baby in her arms, who she had been given responsibility to carry while his parents argued. It was as if he too knew that he had caused a major problem in their home, as he would not be consoled.

After Donald left, Chinyere heard Madam return to her room, where she was to continue sobbing. Baby still cried aloud, and she rose up to rock him and sing to him, but he cried all the more. She wondered if he was hungry and offered him his bottle again. Still, he refused to take it. Eventually, she checked to see if he had soiled himself.

Chinyere carried the boy to his changing station, where she changed his diaper, having been shown only once how to do it. The boy quietened down after that and accepted his bottle. After a feed, he was able to settle in his crib and sleep. She rocked him gently, singing softly. For his sake, if for nothing else, she wished Madam and Oga would make peace again.

***

As much as Chinyere loved Baby, she didn't like the many ways his arrival disrupted her life. It has been almost two months since Madam came home with him, and the dust had finally settled. Things didn't go back to how they had been between Oga and Madam. He rarely spoke with his wife and didn't try to get to know Baby Benjamin either.

Madam was moody as usual. The only thing that made her happy was her son. But she still left Chinyere to do all the nappy changes, baths, bottle feeding and cleaning. She only played with him, and watched him, while Chinyere attended to the house chores. Chinyere often wondered why she had even bothered to adopt a baby she wasn't interested in looking after.

The problem now was that children were resuming school in a couple of weeks, but Chinyere hadn't even sat for any entrance exams. She hadn't had time to study, and she had no idea which school she would be attending. Every time she brought up the issue with Madam, she would tell her to stop worrying, that they would enrol her when the time came. Chinyere was beginning to doubt that she would be going to school, because Madam needed her so much to look after Baby, and she wasn't actively looking for a nanny. Chinyere hadn't even gone for the break she had been promised, because Madam had called her parents to let them know about the baby, and how much she needs Chinyere to help out.

Chinyere knew her only chance at completing her education would be to involve Oga. Things hadn't really been the same between them either. Since he was avoiding Baby, and she was almost always with the boy, she didn't get to see much of Oga. When he did seize the opportunity to see her, in those few occasions Madam took Baby to the hospital for check-ups, it hadn't felt the same. It had only been about him and his need, and she felt used every time. She especially hated how he ignored her and pretended not to know her intimately, whenever anyone else was around.

Chinyere took the opportunity one Saturday, when Madam had to leave for a Women In Business Conference and she was left home alone with Baby and Oga, to bring up the issue about her education with him. Oga was home as usual, but he woke up late today. Chinyere was in the kitchen sterilising Baby's bottles and equipment, when she heard Oga coming down the stairs. She tensed a bit, as she worried how she would raise the issue with him.

She knew he was at the door of the kitchen watching her, but was surprised when he asked, "Chinyere, have you put on weight?"

She turned around and looked at him, before looking down at herself. Her figure was more pronounced, her hips wider, but her weight gain was only slight. She worried if he was asking because he thought she was pregnant. She hoped not, though the pills she took often made her feel bloated. She frowned. "I don't think so."

Donald had been looking at her rounded butt. There was definitely some weight gain there. He had never been an ass man, but he liked it. He moved closer to her and squeezed her bottom when he got next to her. He was surprised when she moved away from him.

"Are you okay?" he asked, only slightly concerned.

Chinyere put down the sponge in her hand, and wiped her

hands with a towel, before putting it on the small dining table in the kitchen. "I'm not, Sir. I need to talk to you..."

"Oh," Donald said, giving her an intent look. He was wondering if she wanted him to stop being intimate with her. He didn't know if or how he would take her rejection if she did, but he prepared himself for it. He was already thinking of other arrangements they could make that would make their relationship more convenient for both of them... "What's wrong?"

"Sir, I want to go to school." Chinyere was downcast.

"But I thought that was settled..."

"No, it's not. Madam never enrol me for school because of Baby! She promised me that I will go to school, and I cannot even read my books again!" Chinyere swallowed. Her fluency was much improved, though she often resorted to broken English, whenever she was stressed or it was convenient.

"Oh... I didn't realise. Don't worry, I'll talk to her, and I'll sort everything out," Donald said, smiling and moving closer to Chinyere.

She looked up at him. "Thank you, Sir." She looked down, uncertain. She didn't know if they could continue their relationship. She liked him, but she didn't want to give up her education to have him. She feared that every time they had sex, she was closer and closer to losing her freedom to study. She'd been taking the pills he had bought for her to take every day. He'd said that they would prevent her from getting pregnant. But she didn't like the side effects. Apart from feeling constantly bloated, her periods were sporadic and her breasts were often tender.

Donald pulled Chinyere into his arms. He looked in her eyes and saw her uncertainty. "Is that all?"

She swallowed. She didn't know how to tell him that she didn't like how he treated her in public. That she didn't like what she was doing with him, and who she had become to him. That she wished they could stop.

However, she wanted to please him. She liked him inside her, though it had initially been painful. She liked knowing that he also wanted to make her happy because of their special relationship. But this wasn't the life she wanted! This wasn't the relationship she wanted with a man. And in a way, she hated him for making her weak...and feel and do these bad things.

She turned from him, hoping her body language would do the talking. But he put two fingers on her chin and turned her to face him. He kissed her lips softly and looked in her eyes. When he got the look of desire that was the signal for him to proceed, he bent his head and claimed her lips in his passionately.

She had doubts, he knew. He had doubts too. But right now, this couldn't be helped. They needed each other.

***

Osinachi returned home to an unusual sight that afternoon. Donald was feeding Benjamin! He hadn't done that since she brought him home eight weeks ago. It almost made her cry. She went to his side and he looked up at her, and she instinctively bent down to kiss him, and then the little boy in his arms.

"Thank you," she muttered, happily.

Donald smiled. "He's beautiful," he said, with emotion.

After their morning session on the kitchen table, Chinyere had asked him why he never carried Benjamin, and he hadn't been able to come up with a good excuse except to say that he didn't want his wife to 'win'. But Chinyere had told him that he was the one losing, and it had just changed everything for him. He hadn't seen it that way before... Not even when Osinachi had said the same thing to him about a month ago.

Osinachi went up to her room, and thanked God for touching her husband's heart. She prayed that her marriage would be healed, and anything that was hindering their happiness would be broken in Jesus' name. As she prayed, she was reminded of the Scripture that said "*Where no counsel is, the people fall: but in the multitude of counsellors there is safety*" (Proverbs 11:14).

She took the lesson that they needed to see a marriage counsellor. There were so many things they were not saying to each other, and they were not treating each other with love. She didn't even know how to talk to him about her challenges at work, not to mention her challenges at home. She was even worried about how to bring this issue of marriage counselling to him and was uncertain how he would take it. When did her husband become a stranger?

As she was praying, she heard the door open, and Donald walked in. She quickly rounded off her prayer, rose up and looked at him. He looked like he wanted to talk to her about something. *Wow, God works fast!*

She wanted to ask him if he was okay, but found herself stuttering, so she stilled, and took in a deep breath. Donald smiled at her and reached out to hold her hand. He led her to the bed, where they both sat down at the edge. He gave a deep sigh, and she swallowed hard.

"Osinachi," he began. "I just want to say...that I'm sorry. For how I have been these past couple of months since you brought Benjamin home."

Osinachi teared up but said nothing. She wiped her eyes and looked at her husband as he continued.

"I was angry... I wish you had told me, but what's done is done. I forgive you for what you did...and I want us to be a happy family."

Osinachi threw her arms around him and kissed his cheek. "Thank you, Donald. Thanks for forgiving me. I'm so sorry it happened that way... But, I love Benjamin, and the moment I saw him, I couldn't regret saying "Yes" to that poor girl..."

Donald nodded. "I know. I understand now. He's quite

enchanting..."

"He is!" Osinachi giggled and smiled. Maybe now was the time to raise the issue of marriage counselling, she thought. But, what if it took them back and they argued? Things seemed to be working out on their own without counselling, she thought.

"There's one other thing..." Donald began.

Osinachi looked in his eyes, her breathing stilled in anticipation.

"We need to get a nanny, so Chinyere can go to school."

Osinachi released her breath. She hadn't expected that he would be thinking of their house help. "Oh... Did she talk to you?"

Donald looked uncomfortable. "Yes... She mentioned it this morning. She's worried because you haven't enrolled her yet."

"But I told her I would! I don't know why she's talking to you about this... What else is she complaining about?"

Donald rubbed his wife's back to calm her down. "Nothing... It wasn't even a complaint. I was the one who asked her about her schooling."

Osinachi nodded and swallowed. "Okay. I was going to send Benjamin to a Creche, while she is at school, and then she would return to look after him in the afternoon. We don't need a nanny."

"But she still needs to study and do her homework," Donald said, a little too loudly. "She can't focus on her studies when she's looking after a baby and cleaning the house too."

Osinachi was quiet. Donald swallowed. He had revealed too much emotion.

"I'm sorry. I didn't mean to raise my voice, but..."

"We need to see a Counsellor," Osinachi said, finally. Her suspicions about her husband and her house help had just been reawakened. She had noticed some strange looks between them but decided to think nothing of it. But the way he had just come to apologise, so that he could ask her to do a favour for their maid was shocking! He wasn't even thinking of her...of their marriage!

Donald was taken aback. But it wasn't totally unexpected. He had been expecting her to say that or even ask for a divorce, with the way things had been deteriorating between them. He swallowed.

"No problem. But we still need a nanny."

Osinachi watched as her husband rose up from the bed and walked out of the room. She put her head in her hands and cried. She had been so blind!

CHAPTER SIX

August 2003. Garki District, Abuja.

Osinachi took Monday off to interview a few nannies. Her friends had given her the names of some reputable agencies in Abuja, and she'd contacted them all on Saturday. She was expecting six women to show up for interviews today. She had specified the age-range she was going for, and also knew the type of woman who she wanted to entrust to look after her home and her child. Preferably, she would be mature and unattractive to look at.

She'd interviewed all six by the early afternoon, and had mentally chosen one, who she would be contacting later to resume work the next day. They had all said they were ready to start work, which was good. The one she liked was an older woman, who had expressed that she would have no problem cleaning too, if Baby would be attending a Creche during the weekdays. Osinachi was surprised at how hard to was to find a nanny who was happy to clean as well. Her house wasn't that big, she thought.

After they left, she called Chinyere to bring Benjamin down for his feed and gave her some wrappers to wash outside. She fed Benjamin and watched as Chinyere got herself ready to go out and wash, gathering the buckets and soaps. When Benjamin was done with his feed, she placed him down in his playpen, and put on his musical toys. Then she went into Chinyere's room to begin to look for any evidence that she was sleeping with her husband.

She was thinking she might find used condom wrappers, or even a tiny piece from a used condom wrapper that could have been neglected when sweeping. She was heartbroken when, instead, she came across an almost empty pack of contraceptive pills! The girl was only 15!!! Why would she have contraceptives? Donald didn't even think it necessary to protect himself - to protect her - from STDs!!! *A whole village girl, who could have been raped by God knows how many men*, Osinachi thought.

Well, Osinachi had tested the girl before they had employed her. But that wasn't the point! He was being careless! He was wicked! If indeed he was the reason she was taking these contraceptives...he was very wicked!

Osinachi didn't know what came over her when she shouted "Chinyere!!! Chinyere!!!" at the top of her lungs.

The girl came back into the house and stood at her bedroom doorway, looking at her madam, who was holding a pack of pills in her hand. She knew that this time, she was wrong. This time, she was caught. And this time, she would be leaving. She had no defence.

Still she spoke, not knowing where her boldness came from. "What are you doing in my room?!"

"Are you seriously asking me that? In my house??? Have you gone mad?!"

"It is my room, Ma. And it is private. You can't..."

Chinyere's ears rang with the dirty slap Osinachi laid on her face. Her jaw dropped in surprise, and she instinctively lifted her hand to the side of her lips where her madam's nails had cut her. To fight or not to fight? But Chinyere knew she could not win this fight. She quickly began to pack her things.

"You wretched girl! You prostitute! How can you repay my kindness this way?! What kind of witch are you???" Osinachi was yelling angrily. She wanted to kill the girl. God help her, she would kill this girl if she doesn't answer for herself right now!

Chinyere said nothing, as she gathered her few things into her bags, and began to head for the door. It was at the door that she realised that she didn't have money to travel, and she would need her wages. She stopped and looked at her angry madam, whose eyes issued death threats at her. She swallowed.

"I need my money," she managed to say, and was shocked to hear Osinachi's laughter.

"You have not answered me! You have not shown me one ounce of respect! You have been sleeping with my husband, and you will not deny it... And you expect me to pay you...? For what?!"

"For my work! I worked for that money!"

"You are a devil! That's what you are... God will judge you! Get out of my house!"

"I'm not leaving unless you pay me!" Chinyere didn't know where she got the audacity to stand and say these things, when her legs were shaking and threatening to give way on her. But she knew that her madam had pride and much more to lose if anyone else found out what had been happening in this house.

Osinachi looked at the girl and her rage got the better of her. She pounced on her. The two ladies fought like a couple of cats, and Chinyere gave as good as she got.

Eventually, sense prevailed, and Osinachi cried out to the security guard, when she had pulled herself away from Chinyere and managed to open the front door. Chinyere resisted them as much as she could, but she had no chance against Ibrahim's strength, as he carried her out of the house and out of the compound. Still, she wouldn't leave the gate, until he returned with a whip to chase her away.

***

Donald was surprised to return home to an empty house. Osinachi had sent a text message saying that she needed to go and spend a couple of days with her mother, because she was ill, and would be taking Baby with her. He had hoped he would at least come home and find Chinyere. Osinachi had not mentioned that Chinyere would be accompanying her, and he hadn't expected that she would.

Donald peeked into Chinyere's room, just to be sure that her things were still there and was surprised to see the state of the room, and that Chinyere's things were not in the closet. Had she gone? Had they been found out? Was that the real reason Osinachi left? He swallowed, wishing he could call Chinyere, but knowing she didn't enjoy the luxury of a mobile phone.

He went up to his room and was relieved to see that his room was in order, and his wife hadn't packed out. But he was still worried about why Chinyere had gone and what Osinachi knew about them. He decided to call his wife to ask her what was going on, but her phone was switched off. He called her parents' landline, and it just rang until it disconnected.

Whatever had happened, he would have to wait and find out. He couldn't go down to Lagos tonight to his in-law's home. Besides, if they wanted him to reach them, Osinachi's phone wouldn't be switched off, and they would have picked his call. And they could always call him back.

He decided he would go out and eat, as there was nothing prepared at home for him. When he got outside, he asked the security guard what time Chinyere had left. That's how he learnt that there had been a fight about 2pm that afternoon, and that Chinyere had been dragged, carried and chased out of his house that day.

"She was beating Madam seriously! If you see Madam's face, eh?! Hmmm... I don't know what kind of wicked child that one is..." Ibrahim said, shaking his head.

Donald was surprised to hear this. Chinyere beating his wife??? What could have led to that? He could hardly believe it, let alone imagine it. He shook his head and thanked Ibrahim, before driving out of the compound.

***

Osinachi was devastated. She'd told her mother everything that had happened today, and how she had been suspecting her husband for months. She told her about how he had held on to anger over her bringing Benjamin home, and only apologised last weekend, so that he could ask her to get a nanny to relieve the burden on their help who he was sleeping with! Mrs Oji speculated that it could have been because of Osinachi's betrayal that he felt he could do what he did and urged her to forgive him.

"But he never confessed!" Osinachi objected. "He came to apologise, and didn't think to confess for this wrong... Our house help, for God's sake! She's just a child!"

"What were you doing with a child working in your home in the first place?!" Mrs Oji rebuked. "I told you before that that thing you are doing isn't good. That girl is supposed to be going to school. Were there not mature girls you could have hired?!"

"Mom, those ones are even more wicked! They are all looking for husbands too, and they won't blink to take a white man for themselves..."

"So, is it because he is white that you were afraid to have a mature girl in your house? Why didn't you hire a house boy then?"

Osinachi shook her head. "Mommy, you are missing the point..."

"Osinachi, you're not listening. The point isn't really who you hired, but who you *married*. Does that man even know

God?"

Osinachi was quiet. They had had this conversation before. Several times actually. Donald was not a religious man. He didn't care about her Faith enough to learn it nor discourage her from it. He always said he didn't need religion to be moral. And she'd believed in his sincerity. That was until the first time he'd cheated on her. And she'd struggled to trust him since.

"Mommy, what can I do now? I've been praying for him...for us. I don't know what to do anymore."

"Do you know what Jesus meant when He said that before you can correct another person, you have to take the log out of your eye first?" Mrs Oji looked at her child pointedly.

Osinachi looked up and was convicted. She knew where her mother was going.

"If you don't know God for yourself... If you are not walking in His will, how can you lead another to Him? You are in this situation, first because of your own sins! When you address that and learn from God what His will is, then you can be able to make corrections in your life... Whether or not your marriage survives is secondary! You just have to get right with God, Osinachi."

Osinachi put her head in her hands. It was the truth, and she knew it. She didn't really feel connected to God. She had been practicing religion all these years, but she didn't know God for herself. No wonder her life could not influence her husband's. If anything, he had influenced her. She'd become very casual about her prayer life and couldn't even remember the last time she had read the Bible.

She began to cry again, and her mother took her into her arms and comforted her. Mrs Oji began to pray over her daughter, calling on the Spirit of God to fall on them. To cleanse, to heal and to restore. To enlighten the way forward, to break every yoke of bondage and bind every contrary power.

They were still praying when the doorbell rang, notifying them of a visitor at 9pm at night. Mrs Oji went to answer it. She was surprised and pleased to behold the man at the door.

"Good evening, Mom," Donald greeted, bending the knee.

Mrs Oji smiled, but wouldn't let him in. Rather, she stepped out. "Good evening, Donald."

"I came for my wife. I heard she was injured."

"I hear you are responsible," Mrs Oji replied, folding her arms across her chest.

Donald bowed his head, grieved. "I'm sorry, Ma. But, I didn't lay a hand on her."

"How could you, Donald? You've hurt her deeper than if you had punched her in the face yourself..."

Donald swallowed. "I know... That's why I'm here. I want to apologise and take my wife home."

"Come back tomorrow. She still needs time."

Donald looked at his mother-in-law, not really knowing what to say. He nodded instead.

Mrs Oji watched as he walked back to the taxi he'd taken from the Airport. She smiled, thinking there was still hope for her daughter's marriage after all. She'd expected him to come after a few days. His visit tonight was encouraging.

"Who was that?" Osinachi asked her mother, curiously.

"Your husband."

"Really? Why did you send him away?"

"First things first... You need time with God. I asked him to come back tomorrow."

"Okay," Osinachi said. She hadn't expected him to come, and she was surprised at how ready she'd been to forgive him and dive back into her marriage, without truly addressing the real issue. Her relationship with God.

CHAPTER SEVEN

Chinwe Ebuka was shocked when she opened her Abuja apartment door at 9:30pm that Monday night to find her niece standing there, unkempt. She opened the door wider to let her in, her thoughts racing as she wondered what could have happened to her.

"What happened to you, Chinyere?" she asked, helping her with her things, which were drenched from the summer rain.

But Chinyere's eyes were dark and spacey. She had barely walked two feet into the apartment when her legs gave way and she collapsed.

Immediately, Chinwe rushed to her and laid her flat on her back, shaking her to see if she would wake up. She called her name severally, before she finally came to. Chinwe hurried to get some water and raised Chinyere up slightly to give her some to drink. After this, Chinyere was supported to lie down on the sofa, while Chinwe went to warm some food for her. She also contacted her parents to let them know that Chinyere had come to her home, and to find out if they knew why.

Mr. and Mrs Chukwuma were clueless as to why Chinyere would have left Mr. and Mrs Peterson's home, to visit her aunty so late at night. Chinwe tried to reach Mrs Peterson, but her number was switched off. No one had Mr. Peterson's number. Chinwe said she would visit the house early tomorrow morning to get to the bottom of this.

When she returned to Chinyere, she was still awake and ate the food offered eagerly. However, Chinyere refused to talk about what had happened to her. She had heard her aunty tell her parents that she would visit the Petersons in the morning. They would all find out the truth for themselves, whether or not she said anything.

***

Osinachi slept in till 8am. She realised that her phone was still switched off and decided to turn it back on, in case of any work-related calls. She got up and went to check on Baby first. She was happy to see that he was already bathed and was being fed by her mother's house help, who had taken charge last night, when Osinachi had arrived.

"Thank you, Doris," Osinachi said, with an appreciative smile. Doris simply nodded and carried on with attending to the baby.

When Osinachi returned to her room, her phone was ringing. She checked the caller ID and saw that it was Ms. Ebuka calling. She hesitated but decided to pick the call.

"Hello?"

"Good morning, Madam."

"Good morning, Ms. Ebuka..."

"Madam, I've been at your house for more than 30 minutes now! Nobody is at home. What happened to Chinyere?"

"You didn't ask her?"

"She said you beat her and threw her out of the house!"

"Look, I am in Lagos. I'll be back in a couple of days. When I come, we can talk."

"What reason could you have for treating a human being like this? Ma, you are not right! We will see you when you come!"

Osinachi took in a deep breath as the line went dead. She didn't even know how to begin to justify herself. This situation had to be properly handled. There was so much at stake, and pointing fingers wasn't going to help anybody here. She got down on her knees and started to pray.

***

Donald arrived at his in-law's place just after twelve noon. He'd spent the night at a hotel and thought he would allow some space before he went back for his wife. He also used the opportunity to catch up on a few things and get updates on how things were going at his office. He hoped he wouldn't meet any resistance today, and that Osinachi would follow him home. He had a meeting in Abuja for tomorrow morning, which he couldn't afford to shift.

Today, it was Mr. Oji who opened the door to Donald. He invited him in, but only as far as the Visitor's Lounge. Mr. Oji called for Doris, who attended to them promptly. She brought a tray of juices and water with two tumblers, before curtsying and leaving them.

Donald shifted uncomfortably in his seat. He knew his father-in-law intended to chat with him, but he didn't know what he could or should say. He had no idea how he would explain his actions, or how much lying he could get away with, because he still didn't know what they knew about what had happened.

When Mr. Oji didn't show any sign of initiating a conversation, he decided to ask instead. "Is Osinachi around?"

Mr. Oji nodded. "Yes. I believe so."

"Is she okay? Can I see her?"

"She's fine. You'll see her soon... She's with her mother."

"Hmmm..." Donald muttered. He stole a glance at his watch. What was this hold-up about?

"Are you in a hurry somewhere?" Mr. Oji asked, a little irritated.

Donald shook his head. "No, Sir... It's not that. I just need to speak with my wife."

"And say what?"

Donald looked into Mr. Oji's eyes, fighting the urge to tell him it was none of his business. But certainly, it had become his business because his daughter had returned home to seek help. He swallowed. "I need to explain myself."

Mr. Oji smiled. "What exactly are you explaining?"

Donald let out a loud sigh. "I don't know what she has told you..."

"Does it matter? You tell me... What's going on?"

"We're just going through a tough time at the moment..." Donald said, looking up briefly to gauge his father-in-law. The man's face revealed nothing. He sighed. "I... I... I really need to talk to my wife."

Mr. Oji's eyes narrowed. "You're not ready to be honest, are you? What are you hiding? What are you protecting?"

Donald picked up his glass and poured himself a drink. He almost downed it in one go. "I'm not hiding anything. I just think some things are private... Between a man and his wife."

Mr. Oji sat back in his chair and assessed his son-in-law. If he had really done what Osinachi said he did, he didn't look sorry. Why was he here? "Do you love my daughter?"

"Of course!"

Mr. Oji raised an eyebrow. "She doesn't know that... So, it's not that obvious." He sighed and decided he would come out with the question he really wanted the answer to. "Is it true that you were sleeping with your house help?"

Donald looked away then. He clenched his jaw, and looked about the room, wondering how else he could answer the question without saying "Yes". Eventually, he nodded, but only slightly.

Mr. Oji just shook his head sadly. "So, what's the explanation for that?"

Donald raised his hands and wiped his palms on his face, to calm himself down. This was gruelling. Confessing to his father-in-law. He looked him in his eyes finally and said honestly. "I have none." He swallowed, before he looked away.

Mr. Oji nodded. "Then what do you want to explain to Osinachi?"

"Sir, I just need her to forgive me. I just want to tell her that I'm sorry..."

Mr. Oji grimaced. "I'm afraid your apologies will mean nothing if you are not truly repentant. I don't think you realise the gravity of what you've done to her... To your marriage. Until you do, you are not ready to fight for her and do what is right..."

"What are you saying, Sir?"

"I'm saying there's no point rushing reconciliation...because this didn't fall apart in one day. If you want a fighting chance, do the hard work of soul-searching. Get to the root of this, and you'll have a chance of growing on a solid foundation. Even if Osinachi goes home with you today, it doesn't mean that your marriage will work. The question I want you to ask yourself is: do you want your marriage to work?"

Donald nodded, and Mr. Oji raised an eyebrow. "Yes, Sir. I do."

"Then give her time. Give yourself time to think about what you have done. Then you will know how to make restitution and prevent it from happening again."

Donald swallowed. "Okay... How much time?"

"As much as you need. If this is what you want, you will make amends."

Donald nodded and rose up. He turned around and let himself out of the house. Was this really what he wanted? He'd just assumed that they would let him take his wife and go. He didn't think he would have to grovel. They didn't even let him see her... But they were right, and he knew it. He didn't really know what he wanted.

***

Osinachi looked out of the window from her bedroom, when she heard the front door shut, indicating that Donald was leaving. She hadn't been able to hear his conversation with her father. She'd expected to be called down, when they were ready for her, and was surprised that he was leaving again. But she also knew she wasn't ready yet.

She was barely thinking straight. Sometimes she wanted him so badly that she wanted to run back home and pretend that none of this ever happened. And other times, she was so mad and so hurt she feared she would kill him if she were face to face with him again.

She kept remembering how vicious Chinyere had been when they had fought. It was so painful to be beaten by the girl her husband had been sleeping with - in her house! God, she still wondered if they had done it on her matrimonial bed. She put one hand to her mouth to hold back a sob, but there was nothing she could do for the aching wound in her heart.

In that moment, Donald looked up at her room window, and she dashed behind the curtain. The last thing she wanted was for him to see her like this. About a minute later, she peeped out again, and saw his taxi pulling out of her parents' large compound. Why hadn't he stayed and fought for her, she wondered? She'd hoped he would.

However, there was still that nagging thought that that wouldn't have been enough, even though she might have given in to her need for him. A band-aid couldn't heal this wound. She needed God, as her mother kept telling her. She needed to get to the point where her joy was found in Him and in no other... And she feared that she still had a long way to go.

***

Chinyere had been in bed all day. She'd hardly slept much

during the night, being traumatized by all she'd suffered the day before. She'd woken up a couple of times screaming, and Chinwe had rushed to her side to calm her down. So today, she had decided to let Chinyere take it easy and rest.

As a Civil Servant, Chinwe often made it home by 6pm. She checked on her niece when she returned from work, and was happy to see that she was awake, though she was still lying in bed. She went to sit beside her and gave her a small smile.

"Have you eaten anything today?" Chinwe asked.

Chinyere nodded.

"What did you eat?"

"Indomie and bread. Thanks."

"That's good. So, are you ready to talk about what happened...?"

Chinyere shook her head, and a tear ran down her cheek. She fought back a sob.

"Are you feeling strong? Or do we need to go to the hospital?"

"No, I'm fine. I just have a headache," she said, and swallowed. She shut her eyes, hoping her aunty would get the message and leave her alone.

"Okay... But all your sleeping will make it worse. Come and watch some TV with me."

Chinyere nodded but made no attempt to get up.

"I didn't meet anyone at the house this morning. Mrs Peterson said she's in Lagos and will be back in a couple of days. We will go together to her house on Thursday."

Chinyere shook her head. "I no fit go back to that house... Abeg, collect my money for me."

Chinwe sighed deeply. This must be really serious, that Chinyere couldn't talk about it, and was too afraid to go back. What kind of people were these Petersons? She couldn't imagine how the set-up could have broken down so irreparably.

"If you want your money, Chinyere, then you had better come with me! I am not your messenger!" Chinwe said at last, knowing that if she really wanted to get the truth, Chinyere would have to accompany her. She arose from the bed and walked towards the door. "So, are you coming to watch TV or what?"

CHAPTER EIGHT

Osinachi returned home on Thursday morning. She preferred to return when she knew Donald would be at work. She wasn't yet ready to see him, and they still hadn't spoken since she'd left home on Monday. She'd contacted the nanny service to request for the woman she had chosen from her interviews on Monday. Fortunately for her, she was still available, and was happy to resume work that Thursday morning as well.

Osinachi still hadn't found a Creche for Benjamin, and decided she would do the search today, so that she could at least get some work done tomorrow. She'd had the worst business week, being mentally unavailable and having to cancel important meetings that could not be rescheduled. She didn't feel completely ready to return home, but she was beginning to feel like she never would be. She'd taken a much-needed time-out to pray and re-evaluate her life and choices, so that she could make the right decision, whether to stay and fight for her marriage or walk away.

The house was surprisingly neat when she let herself in. It was obvious that Donald hadn't been eating at home, as there were only a couple of glasses by the sink. It seemed he had easily adapted to the bachelor's life, and it hurt Osinachi to think that she wasn't missed.

The nanny, Susan, arrived about thirty minutes after Osinachi got home, and got to work immediately. Osinachi talked her through everything, showing her how she sterilised Baby's things, prepared his food and also where and how she handled his personal care. Fortunately, Benjamin was napping, so Susan could attend to some cleaning, while Osinachi took some time to rest in her room.

As she laid in bed, silent tears streaming down her face, Osinachi remembered the Bible study she'd had with her mother last night. They had studied the book of Romans, as her mother had used select scriptures to minister to her about what Jesus Christ had done to redeem the world from the power of sin. Yesterday's memory verse was taken from Romans Chapter 8:

"*the carnal mind is enmity against God: for it is not subject to the law of God, neither indeed can be...*" (verse 7).

"There are only two types of people, Osinachi. Those who are born of the Spirit, and those who are not. Those who are not born of God's Spirit cannot be subjected to His laws... They cannot be righteous, and you shouldn't expect them to be. I know you are surprised by what Donald did, but I am not. The carnal man is capable of anything. The Bible also says in Jeremiah seventeen verse nine that "*the heart of man is deceitful above all things, and desperately wicked. Who can know it*"? That's just the truth! If not for God's Spirit in me that constrains me and illuminates the right way for me to go, I know I am capable of anything...

"I know you can't help but take it personal, but this thing he has done is not about you. It's about him. He needs God, and until he surrenders to God, you cannot and shouldn't expect him to do right by you. He may try, and many men do try, but it takes God to love sacrificially. And you need God too. You need to surrender to His will and let Him teach you how to love...and how to live.

"When you get home, I hope you will remember this, and consider how you relate and communicate with Donald. You cannot change a man with accusations or even with rebuke. Only God can change a man! If you really love him, and have forgiven him, and want to make your marriage work, then you need to return home as a Minister in that house. You have to be ready to die to yourself every day, as long as God calls you to serve in this marriage.

"Don't relent in praying for him. Don't stop forgiving him. Don't hold back love and respect for him. It will be hard, especially if he isn't repentant. It will be very hard. But never forget that you can do all things through Jesus Christ who is your strength! Do you believe that?"

Osinachi sobbed. "God help me!" she cried aloud, as her body was overtaken with sobs. "Lord, I need You to take control... Please... I can't do this without You. Please touch my husband's heart... Please, God! Save him!!!"

***

"*When are you coming home?*"

The text message from Donald came in unexpectedly, as Osinachi was about to leave to visit the local Creches later that afternoon. She felt both excited and annoyed by the text, especially since it was the first one he had sent since she'd left home. She decided to text back. "*I came back this morning.*"

"*Okay. I'll see you tonight,*" was his response.

Osinachi flipped her phone shut and put it away in her bag. She didn't understand his unemotional response. He hadn't even texted to say he was sorry. *God, give me grace*, she prayed silently.

"*I missed you.*"

Osinachi rolled her eyes but couldn't help the warmth that crept into her heart when she saw that text from Donald. She'd brought out her phone to save the contact details of one of the Creches she had liked. A small smile lifted her lips, and she shut her eyes for will power. She wouldn't reply his text. They still had much to talk about.

***

Donald had been thinking a lot about what Osinachi's father had said. It seemed that the ball was in his court, and it was all up to him, to fight for his marriage or walk away. Having had the house to himself for a couple of days, he had been able to reflect and think about his actions, and what he really wanted. It certainly wasn't to keep up an affair with his maid.

He'd never thought that he would be that kind of a man. He hated men like that, who took advantage of vulnerable women and girls. He always hated it whenever he watched or read stories about the Transatlantic Slave Trade and learnt about the horrible way black girls and women were objectified and abused. He had even denied his attraction to Osinachi for months, because he thought maybe he was responding to some primitive desire to own a black slave.

When she'd brought Chinyere home last year, she had been so innocent looking and he hadn't regarded her as a threat in any way. They had had house helps before, and a couple of them had been desirable to look at, but he'd never entertained such thoughts, nor even thought to follow through with any ideas. He couldn't understand why he had taken exception to Chinyere. After that night when he'd shared his sandwiches with her, he hadn't been able to stop noticing her. And he had noticed and appreciated the way she'd also changed towards him.

He really hadn't planned to sleep with her. It was a case of risk meeting opportunity, and him not being strong enough to resist temptation. *She'd even been the one to make the first move, hadn't she?* Sure, he could have turned her down, but he was only a man... Damn, he should have just sent that girl packing the moment he felt the first attraction for her! He should have let Osinachi fire her that day... He should have been stronger...and better!

Donald beat his head against his palm repeatedly as he scolded himself for the mess he had gotten himself into. He had no idea how to begin to make amends to Osinachi. He had no clue what she knew about the affair. Had Chinyere confessed everything? Had she even confessed at all? Or was Osinachi acting on suspicions?

Well, the truth was out now, because he had confessed his guilt to the charge of sleeping with his maid to his father-in-law. He figured Osinachi now knew that much. But maybe she didn't need to know everything. Maybe there was some way to explain it to her... If she didn't know the facts, he could blame it on his anger about the baby... Say it was a one-time slip up or something... *Oh, shiiiit!* What had he done?

Just tell the whole truth. Donald didn't like that advice at all. He shuddered, as if to shake the spirit that uttered that piece of wisdom away. What was the truth going to do? He would simply apologise. And beg her until she forgave him. He knew she would. She'd forgiven him before. She would do anything for him and their home, he was sure of it. He just had to show her that he was sorry, and that it had meant nothing.

Donald decided to leave work early to go home. If Osinachi was up for it, maybe he could take her out to dinner tonight. He stopped by at a flower shop and got her some flowers. He hoped he wouldn't have to grovel... He smiled to himself, feeling hopeful.

***

Chinyere stood at the gate with her aunty feeling nervous. Ibrahim had gone to verify from Madam that they could enter. At least they knew she was home. After what seemed like an unnecessarily long time, he returned to open the small gate and let them in. Chinyere avoided his gaze, which she felt the heat of, as she walked past him.

Osinachi opened the door to them, and Ms. Ebuka walked in first. Chinyere tried to still her shakes. She didn't know why she felt so shaky and intimidated. All she wanted was her money. She didn't know what Ms. Ebuka wanted, and she hoped she had no intention of making her continue her work for the Petersons. She liked Oga, but she knew there was no future for her here.

Madam sat down on the armchair in the living room, while Chinyere and Chinwe sat on the sofa. They waited for the new maid to drop the tray of water and juices she had brought, with three glasses. The big-boned woman started to lay out coasters on the coffee table, getting ready to ask for orders, when Madam raised her hand for her to leave.

At that moment, a car horn sounded, indicating that Donald had returned home. Osinachi took in a deep breath. She wasn't sure if this was the best way for her to meet her husband after almost four days. But she knew that she really didn't want to have this meeting with these people by herself.

"That's my husband. I think we might as well wait for him to join us..." Ms. Ebuka nodded her agreement.

Osinachi opened the door to Donald and was only slightly surprised to see that he was holding flowers. She was immediately irritated by the embarrassed smile on his face. Did he really think it would be that easy? She stepped back so he could enter and didn't take the flowers from him.

"Osinachi, I'm sorry," he said, when he'd shut the door behind himself. He reached for her hand, but she pulled it free.

"We have company, Donald," she said, feeling her chest tighten. The pain was taking hold of her again. She mustered all her strength to keep herself together. She couldn't fall apart in front of Chinyere and her aunty. She turned her back to him as she led the way back to the sitting room.

Donald's face fell. *Company?* Did her parents come with her? Or had she told his mother? Whose presence could be more important than handling the issues between them, and mending their marriage? He dropped the bouquet of flowers on the entrance table before he entered the living area.

Donald was shocked when he saw Chinyere sitting on the sofa with a strange woman. Was that her mother? Had she told her mother that he had slept with her? Why were they here? How serious had this gotten? It was consensual sex, and the only person he had hurt was his wife... *Wasn't it?*

He looked into Chinyere's eyes, hoping that they would respond with an understanding...an apology...an explanation. But Chinyere simply looked away. Then he looked at the woman with her. Her narrow eyes studied him.

Donald went to sit on the arm of the chair his wife was sitting on, gathering his wits. "Ummm... Good evening, Madam. What is this visit about?"

CHAPTER NINE

"Three nights ago, my niece showed up at my doorstep soaking wet and looking like she'd run into some thugs, who had beaten her mercilessly! She fainted moments later. How she got to my house, I don't even know. Why she left your house, I still don't know. She is clearly traumatised and hasn't been able to say anything other than she had to leave, because she could not live with you anymore. I just want to know what's been happening here and why you would let her leave your house without even talking to me first!"

Donald swallowed. He looked at Chinyere, who was still avoiding his gaze. He looked down at his wife, who shifted uncomfortably in her seat. From the woman's account, it was evident she didn't know anything, and he wished she would leave none the wiser. He wished Chinyere would look at him so that he could be sure their secret was safe.

"I'm sorry about how Chinyere left this house," Osinachi finally spoke up. "I don't know what must have happened or how she got to your house, but I admit that I fought with her the day she left. I had just discovered some birth control pills in her room, and I was very angry with her, because she was rude to me when I asked her about it. I don't understand what a fifteen-year-old girl would be doing with contraceptives, or how she even got them."

Donald decided to play dumb and watch. So far, Chinyere hadn't said anything and he hoped she would continue to hold her tongue. But he wasn't going to be that lucky tonight...

"Contra-wetin??? Chinyere?! What are you doing with contraceptives?! Are you having sex???" Chinyere looked down and away until her aunty's hand smacked her head hard. "Answer me! Are you stupid?!"

Chinyere nodded and swallowed. "Yes, Ma... Oga gave me..."

Osinachi felt her heart break at Chinyere's confession. She had known. Well, she had suspected, and had held on to reasonable doubt. But with the confession, she now had to face the truth of Donald's betrayal. *Again?!* She shifted away from him slightly and avoided eye contact with anyone, afraid that she would cry.

Ms. Ebuka's gaze instantly met Donald's, whose expression was still hard to decipher. "You gave her pills???"

"She told me she had a boyfriend... And I told her that condoms weren't 100% safe..." Donald surprised himself with how quickly the lie came out.

Ms. Ebuka's narrowed eyes returned to her niece again. She could smell a fish. She gave Chinyere another hard slap. "You have a boyfriend?!"

Osinachi's heart was beating fast. She looked at Chinyere, wishing and willing her to confess that she had a boyfriend, and that she'd jumped to conclusions when she'd accused her of sleeping with her husband. God, she wished the girl would just come out with the whole truth!

Donald was also staring hard at Chinyere, his eyes dark and begging. Nobody needed to know what happened between them. Chinyere opened her mouth to speak, and Donald found himself interrupting her. "Please, don't be upset with her... I'm sorry I said anything...and I'm sorry I gave her the pills. I was just being protective of her... You never know what these kids are getting up to, these days… And it's always better to be safe."

Everyone was looking at him now, and he realised that he was rambling and sweating. He ran a hand through his thick hair, nervously. "Look, Chinyere's a lovely girl, but she wasn't a good fit for us. She and Osinachi never got along. I think this whole thing was one big misunderstanding. I wasn't home when she left, otherwise I would have made sure she was driven home safely. I'm sorry. We're sorry." He eventually stopped and swallowed.

Ms. Ebuka's mouth slowly dropped as she gaped at the guilt-stricken white man before her. "You were sleeping with her!" she accused.

Osinachi's heart constricted, and she sucked in a gasp. *So, it was indeed that obvious.* She hadn't made a hasty leap to conclusion. She looked up at her husband, who had stood up, and was rubbing his hand through his golden-brown hair. Was he finally going to confess? Could she stand to hear him try to hide the truth again?

"No... Of course not!" he lied.

"You are a liar! You've been sleeping with my niece!" Ms. Ebuka stood up, surer of herself than ever. She looked down at Chinyere. "Did he force you? You can tell us... He can't do anything to you now."

Chinyere shook her head. "He didn't force me..."

"But you slept with him, sha?" Ms. Ebuka asked.

Chinyere nodded.

Ms. Ebuka restrained herself from beating her niece senseless in front of her former Bosses. She would deal with her at home. She looked at the man, and then his wife, whose expression was distant. She pitied the woman. She could now imagine the fight that would have happened at the time she'd discovered that her house help had been sleeping with her husband. She returned her gaze to the wicked man.

"You! *Oyibo!* You do not have shame! You think you can sleep with anybody you like because you are oyibo, se?! She's a child! You bastard! You will not get away with this! Chinyere, let's go!"

"Please... Please... I'm sorry," Donald begged, trying to block their exit.

"You're not sorry enough! Chinyere! Get up, let's go!"

Chinyere rose up and followed her aunty. She remembered why she had come along. "Aunty, I want my money..."

Ms. Ebuka stopped and turned around. "Yes... We want her money!" she said, folding her arms across her chest.

"No problem... I'll pay her salary, even two months' salary..."

"*Two months' salary?*"

"Six months...?" Donald was bargaining.

Ms. Ebuka's eyebrows shut up. This man was trying to bribe them?! Could she be bribed? "One million naira and I won't call the Police."

Donald froze. He hadn't expected that. *She is just a maid*...he thought. N1,000,000??? He became angry. "It was *consensual*!"

"She cannot give consent, you idiot! She's underaged!"

"The age of consent is 11 years in Nigeria..."

Ms. Ebuka laughed. "Well, since The Child's Rights Act came into Law last month, it is a CRIME to have sex with a child! A child is ANYONE under the age of 18 years! And the penalty for child sexual abuse is life imprisonment! See you in Court!"

Ms. Ebuka grabbed Chinyere's hand and headed determinedly towards the door.

"You're lying..." Donald gasped. If this was true, he was screwed! He couldn't go to prison! *Not in Nigeria!*

"I work for the Ministry of Women's Affairs. In fact, I think I will just call my Boss now..."

"Jeez... Wait! Ummm... *N200,000. Please...*"

"N1,000,000..."

"N500,000. I'm begging you!"

Ms. Ebuka brought out her phone and began to dial a number.

"Okay... Okay. I'll pay N1,000,000. You will accept a cheque?"

Ms. Ebuka nodded. She looked at Chinyere from the corner of her eyes and tried to hide her smile. The girl was proving profitable after all. She kept her hands folded across her chest and stared hard at Mrs Peterson, as Mr. Peterson fumbled in his suitcase for his cheque book.

***

Donald shut and locked the door after Chinyere left with Ms. Ebuka, and just leaned on it for a moment, uttering a silent prayer even though he didn't believe in God. He thought it couldn't hurt to pray, though he was sure that if there was a God, this would be the one prayer He wouldn't answer! *Please God, don't let them call the Police!* How could he have been so stupid?!

He slowly straightened and turned around, thinking he would see his wife still standing there, but found the room empty. He swallowed. He hadn't expected the night to turn out like this at all.

He picked up his suitcase and walked slowly up the stairs to his bedroom, thinking she would be there. She was not. She must be with the baby. He dropped his suitcase and went and knocked on the door of the nursery. But it was Susan who opened the door with Benjamin in her arms, holding a soiled diaper in one hand. He raised his hand in apology for the disturbance before retreating to keep looking for his wife. Where could she be?

"Osi! Osi baby... Where are you?" he called after her, using a shortened endearing version of her name, he rarely used these days. "Please...come out. Let's talk. Please."

That was when he heard her loud guttural sobs. He followed the sound to the guest bathroom downstairs, which was locked. He leaned against it, feeling remorseful over his actions.

"I'm sorry, Osi. I am so sorry... I don't even know what to say... Please forgive me!"

Her cries reduced in volume, but he could still hear her sniffing and whimpering as she tried to pull herself together.

"Baby, it didn't mean anything... It was a mistake. I was just angry with the baby situation and I didn't..."

"LIAR!!!" Osinachi shouted from inside the bathroom, as she cried aloud. "You're such a lying bastard! Stop it! Stop lying to me!"

Donald closed his mouth and placed his hand on the door. "Osinachi... I don't know what the truth is... I know what I did was wrong and I know I will never do that again... I don't know why I did it...but I know that I love you... And I'm sorry. That's all I know. I wish... I wish..." He shut his eyes, trying to speak the truth, but thinking that it was still not the complete truth. "I wish it never happened, Osi. I wish I never hurt you. Please, I need you to forgive me."

Osinachi opened the door, startling Donald, who had been leaning on it. She squeezed past him and pulled her hand free when he tried to grab it. She rushed past him and hurried up the stairs. She slammed the bedroom door shut and locked it when she got in.

Donald knocked and tried to open it, before giving up and leaning against it. "I know you still love me, Osi. I know that's why you came back. I know you believe in us...and that we will get through this. I believe in you, Baby. I believe in us too. I want you to know I'll do everything I can to make us happy again... *Whatever it takes.* This is not the end of us, Osi... I love you."

***

Osinachi shut her eyes and tried to shut out his words.

She didn't know what to believe. He had been determined to keep lying. If Chinyere and her aunty hadn't come tonight, would she even know the truth today? Would he have fed her a lie that she would have readily believed, so that they could be happy again?

She knew she desperately wanted to believe in his good intentions, and professions of love for her. She desperately wanted them to be happy, to be the perfect couple, but now she knew that they would never be. How could they get through this?

It was bad enough that he had cheated on her! It was awful that he had carried on an affair! It was despicable that he had done it under her nose...in her house...with their maid! But it seemed unforgivable that he had taken advantage of a child, and now stood in peril with the Law!!!

Even if she could forgive him, what would happen if and when the world found out? When everyone discovered that not only was her marriage far from perfect, but that her husband was a paedophile! A child sex offender! How could she even sleep with him again? Why had he done something so terrible??! Was she that horrible a wife?

Osinachi sobbed into the pillow to quieten her cries. She remembered what her mother had said about the carnal nature of man, and how she shouldn't take her husband's actions personally. But it was hard not to. It was so hard not to think that if only she had done things differently, this wouldn't have happened.

She wished she could say that he was ignorant of his actions, like Jesus did when He was crucified and said "*Father forgive them for they know not what they do...*" But Donald clearly knew what he was doing! He had bought her birth control pills, which meant it wasn't a one-off, but an ongoing affair he planned to continue. He had even said that he thought the age of consent was eleven years in Nigeria. *This was something he had thought about and even researched!*

Osinachi could feel herself getting angry again. She thought she had forgiven him and was ready to move past it to work on her marriage, but today had only made it more obvious to her that she didn't know her husband at all. And she didn't know if he was worth laying down her life for. In fact, she was quite sure that not only did he expect her to, but he would watch her give up everything for him, and not even show any gratitude for her sacrifice. What kind of *monster* did she marry?

CHAPTER TEN

Donald could hear the sirens from a mile away. He looked out of his bedroom window and saw the police cars as they drove on his street and parked outside his house. *They were here!* Ms. Ebuka had called the police!

Donald panicked. They had already blocked the gate, and several officers were entering the compound. The next thing he heard was banging on the front door. "Don't get it! Don't open the door!" he shouted, but Osinachi ignored him and went to open the door.

Hastily, he climbed out of the window, before remembering his fear of heights. He clung to the ledge and climbed up to the roof of his house. He had no idea where he was running to, but he couldn't be caught. He couldn't go to prison!

He heard one of the police officers shout, "He's on the roof!" and he began to run! He didn't know where he got the strength to jump over to the next compound, but he landed on the wide balcony, knocking a table and a couple of chairs down with his fall. The police were on his tail. He jumped on one of the white marble beams that held up his neighbour's house and slid down it.

He quickly ran to the backyard, when the security guard

shouted after him. At the backyard, there was a field and a bushy area. He ran into the bushes until he got to the hedge that fenced the property in. There was an opening in the hedge, and he slid past it. He could hear some feet on his trail. He heard a man say, "He went this way!"

Donald quickly found a place to hide in the thick bush and waited. The sound of feet was getting louder now... They passed him, and he breathed out a sigh of relief. But it was a little too soon, because someone pulled back the shrub behind which he was hiding and he screamed.

***

"What are you doing in the closet?"

"Osinachi! Thank God! Have they gone?"

"Have who gone?"

"The Police!!! Are they still at the house?!"

Osinachi looked at her husband, who was cowering in his closet, looking like a little child, and could barely believe her eyes. *What game did he think he was playing?* Was this some sort of desperate cry for attention? "Donald, are you okay? There's no Police here!"

"*Don't believe her!*" "*It's a trick!*" "*She's lying!*" "*She's one of them!*" the voices came all at once, and Donald cowered all the more. "Go away!" he cried. "You're going to let them catch me!"

Osinachi swallowed, and lowered herself, realising that Donald really believed people were after him. He was being paranoid over his criminal act, and now lived in fear of getting caught. She spoke softly. "Donald, no one is here but me, Baby and Susan. You're fine. Please come out of the closet."

Donald looked unsure, but slowly stood up and got out of the closet. He rubbed his hand through his hair, and looked back at the open field, only to see a bunch of clothes hanging in the closet. What was happening to him?

He walked slowly to sit on the bed. That was when he

realised that he was in the spare room. He had slept there last night, when Osinachi had locked him out of their bedroom. He hadn't taken his pills yesterday night.

Osinachi watched him as he sat on the bed. It was 8:30am, and he hadn't bathed nor had breakfast. She'd only thought to check on him before leaving for work herself. She really hadn't wanted to, but she was concerned that she hadn't seen nor heard from him that morning and thought maybe he had overslept.

"I guess you're not going to work today..." Osinachi said, looking at her husband, who still looked like a frightened child.

Donald nodded, downcast. "I will... I'll be fine."

"Okay... I have to go now. I'm taking Benjamin to his Creche. Bye."

Donald watched her leave, even as he felt a dark cloud looming over him. He slumped unto the bed, feeling dizzy. He needed to take his medicine.

***

Osinachi had worried about Donald that morning but was finally able to get her mind in her work. She had so much to catch up on. She'd set her alarm for 2pm to remind her to go and pick up Benjamin from the Creche. However, she was very annoyed when it rang, not realising how fast the time had been spent.

This Creche business was going to be disruptive. She really hadn't thought of the challenge of finding good daycare for her baby, when she had been desirous to have one. She got to the Creche by 3pm, due of some traffic, and had to pay for late pick-up, which was further annoying.

She eventually got home at about 3:15pm. She was surprised to see that Donald's car was still in the driveway and wondered what he would still be doing at home. She pressed the bell because she had her hands full with Baby, but no one came to the door. She pressed it again and waited another minute, before struggling to get her keys from her handbag and letting herself into the house.

"Susan!" she called for her nanny. The house was in a state. Hadn't she cleaned up? Where the hell was she? "Susan!!!"

She wandered into the kitchen and was perplexed to see the fridge ajar and almost devoid of food. It looked like someone had ransacked her kitchen and emptied the contents in the bin, which was full and uncovered. Osinachi became angry.

What in God's name was this about? The agency came highly recommended! And where was Donald? How could he have allowed this to happen while he was at home?!

Osinachi dropped Baby down in his playpen in the living room and went to Susan's room. *I better not find her sleeping in the middle of the day, otherwise, she's so fired!* Osinachi opened the door to find the room empty. This was really bizarre! What was going on???

Now afraid that she would find Susan and Donald in the act of adultery, Osinachi anxiously went up the stairs. No, he wouldn't do it… No, he wasn't that cruel! Not when he had just been found out for cheating with Chinyere. *God, please, he can't be this wicked*, Osinachi swallowed as she opened her bedroom door. It was just as she'd left it.

She sighed in relief but was still very perplexed. She decided to call the agency to complain but was shocked by what she heard. They said that they had received a call from Susan, who had been chased out of the house by Mr. Peterson, that morning. *What's the matter with Donald?!*

"Donald!!!" Osinachi yelled at the top of her lungs. Where could he be, and what was he up to? She began to dial his number. She could hear the ringtone very clearly. He was in the spare room. She tried the door. It was locked. She banged on it.

"Donald?! Donald?! Open up! What's the matter with

you?!" she shouted. "This is not funny! The house is in a horrible state and the agency said you threw Susan out! Will you stop being childish and come out for God's sake?! I have to get back to work! *What's gotten into you?!*"

When she didn't get a reply after another minute, Osinachi ran downstairs to get the security guard. He confirmed that Oga hadn't left the house that day, and that Susan had left just after 11am. They both went up to the room. Ibrahim picked the lock on the door and they opened it to see Donald sprawled on the bed, an empty bottle of pills by his side. Osinachi screamed.

***

Osinachi waited anxiously at the Accident and Emergency Unit of their family hospital in Abuja, as Donald was wheeled away to have his stomach pumped. She'd taken the empty bottle with her, in case it was important to determine how to treat him, and maybe they could explain what the pills were for. She'd read the label on the bottle and was shocked when she saw all the warnings about its side effects and against overdoses. She was alarmed to read the word "psychosis" in the description of the drug. What was Donald doing with drugs for the treatment of *psychosis*?

She was soon called in to see a consultant at the hospital. He was a psychiatrist who dealt with such mental health cases, and patients who came into the A&E for attempted suicide. He asked her a few questions to identify the circumstances surrounding the incident, and to determine if this was an accidental overdose or if her husband was prone to or at risk of committing suicide. Osinachi struggled with how to answer the questions honestly, because she didn't want to betray his trust, and possibly jeopardize his freedom by admitting that he had committed an act worthy of imprisonment. She was also embarrassed that she knew so little about his condition and the history behind it.

"Doctor, please... Can you just tell me what is the matter

with my husband? What are those pills for?"

"That is also what I am trying to ascertain, Madam," Doctor Iduta said. "These are anti-psychotics and are usually given for the treatment of severe mental illness, such as schizophrenia and bipolar disorder. Your husband doesn't have a mental health record with this hospital, and he wasn't prescribed these pills by any of the doctors here, so we can't be sure what his diagnosis is. However, from what you have described, it appears that your husband is suffering from paranoid schizophrenia..."

"*Huh?* What is schizophrenia?"

"Schizophrenia is a chronic mental disorder characterized by abnormal social behaviour and failure to understand reality. Common symptoms include false beliefs, unclear or confused thinking, hearing voices that others do not hear, reduced social engagement and emotional expression, and a lack of motivation (s). If your husband is diagnosed with this illness, it is very important for you to know all you can about it, and how you can care for him. Here are some booklets for you to read for more information."

Osinachi took the booklets from the consultant and swallowed. "But how is it that I have never seen him behave this way before...? He never even told me about it..." Osinachi was getting teary. Why did Donald hide this from her? How could he hide this from her? Did he think she wouldn't love him if she knew of his condition? How debilitating was it?

"The symptoms often come on gradually and can be triggered by environmental as well as genetic factors. Because he has been taking medication for it, it is possible that this is something that has been a problem for him for years. Often, it shows up in adolescence, and when well treated, patients can live a pretty normal life, with few relapses. But it isn't enough to take medication. Treatment works best when patients also receive therapy, and also engage in group therapy. Do you know if your husband has been seeing a private therapist?"

Osinachi shook her head. "No... But, I can check his phone in case he has a number saved for a therapist... Maybe his mother will know. I already called her to let her know I was taking him in to the hospital."

"Yes. If she could come, I'd love to ask her some questions too. She would know his medical history. She might also know the name of his therapist, if he has one."

"Well, she's in Lagos. You can speak with her on the phone."

"That's good," Doctor Iduta smiled and watched as Osinachi made the phone call.

***

She should be angry with him. She should be mad as hell! Why did he try to take his life?! After ruining her happy life, wrecking their marriage, and he wants to just sneak out of the picture?! Was he not man enough to face the consequences of his actions? Did he only think of himself???

Osinachi cried, as she looked at her husband laying comatose on his hospital bed. They had done all they could for him. Time would tell if he would pull through. If he was really suicidal, he wouldn't, because dying would be his intention. And in these precious moments, even after the horrible way he had treated her, and cheated on her...even the horrible thing he had done being so secretive and hiding this part of himself from her, she still wanted him to live. Because she loved him.

She took his hand in hers and willed him to come back to her so that they could get through this together. She'd done some reading on schizophrenia and had been so overwhelmed with what she'd read. She was worried that she couldn't cope. That they couldn't cope. But he had lived a normal and happy life up till now. It was only that they hadn't been completely open with each other. And she was also to blame.

She knew that if they could just be first honest with themselves, then honest with each other, they could have the deeply intimate marriage they had always longed for. She cried over him. "If this was your desperate attempt to force me to forgive you, it was horribly wicked of you...but all the same I love you and I forgive you. Donald, please wake up and let's fight this together."

Moments later, Osinachi heard the first beep. Then another. And then another. She looked up at the heart monitor, before she noticed that his eyes were opening.

"Doctor!" she cried happily.

CHAPTER ELEVEN

"Are you helping God?" the preacher asked the congregation. "I will repeat myself, for those who may be hard of hearing… *Are you helping God?!* Are you doing your little bit by faith, or trying to act in the place of God too?"

Osinachi, who had been previously distracted, raised her head up to pay attention. The preacher was a visiting pastor to her Church. Just from the question he'd asked, she knew the message was for her.

"I hear people say all the time that God helps those who help themselves. And I always ask them to show me where that is written in scripture. Many believe these things, not truly understanding the spirit behind them. The spirit of rebellion. The lying spirit of the enemy, which is to steal your faith and trust in God…

"Does God want us to sit around doing nothing for ourselves and waiting for Him to do everything? No, of course not! God calls us *first* to LISTEN! *Listen* people! To listen! Many of us do not listen. We do not know the importance of listening and waiting on the word of the Lord! We are so filled with our own words and ideas and desires, that we plough ahead, and only remember to ask God to bless our plans, when we are getting frustrated! If we had listened, we wouldn't be frustrated."

Sounds of awe and praise arose from the congregation as many were moved by the ministration. Osinachi swallowed. She'd never really thought about listening to God. Praying, she knew about. But this was the first preacher to emphasise the need to listen.

"Are you listening? If you are listening to God, you will hear what He says... And after you have heard Him, He expects you to OBEY? To do what?"

"Obey!" The congregation shouted.

"He expects you to TRUST AND OBEY. They go together. This duo is your faith at work. This is what is pleasing to God; that we trust Him and we obey Him. But first, we must seek Him; seek His will by listening. The Bible says "*Faith cometh by hearing and hearing of the word of the Lord!*" We ought to wait for Him, believing that He exists and He is willing and able to reward all those who put their faith in Him. Are you with me?"

"Yes," Osinachi said, along with majority of those in the congregation. This was definitely a word for her.

"It is written: "*Behold, all ye that kindle a fire, that compass yourselves about with sparks: walk in the light of your fire, and in the sparks that ye have kindled. This shall ye have of mine hand; ye shall lie down in sorrow...*" That is from the book of Isaiah, chapter fifty verse eleven. Check your Bibles. Don't rely on me but verify every teaching for yourself. God is addressing all of us who move ahead to enlighten our own way, without seeking or even *disregarding* His counsel. He is warning us that peril awaits us in our willfulness.

"It is funny how many of these people even try to bribe God with tithes and all sorts of offerings. They are not walking in the will of God. They have not sought His face nor heard His voice. They are following the counsels of men, sowing seeds on fallow ground, directed by false prophets, promising lies for greedy gain, because they *think* that the blessing of God is for sale!"

"Yeehhh!" someone shouted in the congregation. "This is the truth!" another person sounded. Others were quiet, especially the General Overseer and his team of pastors, who hadn't expected this rebuke on some of their teachings and practices.

"Repent and you shall receive mercy," the preacher continued. "I know I am rubbing a few people the wrong way, but it is time for you to know the truth, so that you can be free and receive the blessing of God, which is freely given to all who have faith in Him. Woman, you do not have to pay any man of God seed offering to conceive! Man, you do not have to pay any man of God seed offering to find a wife! Brethren, as long as you are in Christ, you are no longer under a curse… You are blessed! And when you know that, when you believe that, you will begin to see the blessing of God in your life."

Osinachi wiped tears from her eyes and looked at her neighbours. Some were nodding, some were emotional, and others were indifferent. She returned her gaze to the preacher.

"Let me tell you something… God doesn't need your sacrifices; tithes nor offerings. Jesus Christ, the Son of God, has already come and fulfilled the Law and paid the sacrificial price for you! God wants your surrender. Your humility. Your *obedience*. It was for this sin of arrogance that Saul was rejected as King of Israel. Turn your Bibles with me to First Samuel, chapter fifteen, verses twenty-two to twenty-three.

"It is written: "*And Samuel said, hath the Lord as great delight in burnt offerings and sacrifices, as in obeying the voice of the Lord? Behold, to obey is better than sacrifice, and to hearken than the fat of rams. For rebellion is as the sin of witchcraft, and stubbornness is as iniquity and idolatry. Because thou hast rejected the word of the Lord, he hath also rejected thee from being king.*" You see, Saul had been commanded by God to destroy all the Amalekites, but he thought he knew better. And he thought he could offer God an offering from the fruit of his disobedience. How many Sauls do we have in this house?"

Everyone remained silent, and the preacher continued.

"Now, note this question that Samuel the prophet asked: "*Does the Lord delight in burnt offerings and sacrifices, as in obeying His voice?*" Even in the Old Covenant, God preferred obedience to sacrifice. He preferred mercy to sacrifice. The true sacrifice God seeks is a broken and contrite spirit. This, He will never refuse! Now, in the New and Better Covenant, we do not walk by the light of the Old Covenant but live by the Spirit of God, which will lead us into all truth. Jesus said "*My sheep hear My voice and they obey!*" John ten verse twenty-seven. We must be attentive to His voice.

"Children of God, are you listening? Jesus said that "*unless you become as little children, you shall not enter the Kingdom of God*". Children are humble and obedient to their Father. They also trust and rely on Him. If you have been doing things your own way, and are asking for God to bless your plans, you have it all wrong. You are walking in the way of deception and frustration. God has already prepared the way for you to walk in. It is for you to learn it, walk in it and abide by it."

Osinachi took in a deep breath and released it slowly. Though she was convicted by the message, she also felt like a huge weight had been taken off her shoulders. However, she still had questions. Lots of questions. She listened as the preacher continued his sermon about living by faith. And when the sermon was through, she rededicated her life to God, with a renewed passion to know Him intimately.

***

That Sunday, as Osinachi drove home, she thought of her life and the choices she had made. Even while claiming to know and love God, she lived contrary to His commandments. She lived with only one person in control of her life - herself. And everything else she did for God was sacrifice. And not the sacrifice God had called her to make - that of a humble spirit - but the sacrifice of disobedience.

Her good works, offerings, charity and praise were her penance for living for herself, by herself. She was practicing religion, like many others in the Church, but she didn't truly love God. She didn't love Him nor His ways enough to submit and obey.

She hadn't listened to her mother when she'd counseled her against dating Donald, because he was an unbeliever. She'd accused her mother of being judgmental and self-righteous. She'd even said that Donald was a good man, with a good heart and probably more right with God than the majority of those in Church! And to that, her mother had responded, "*No one is good, except God alone*", quoting Mark 10:18.

Now, she knew just how true that was. Before Donald had confessed to her about his infidelity the first time, she'd suspected him many times. She'd even spied on him and sought to catch him in the act, but he'd covered his tracks well and denied every accusation. Until the day he was forced to confess because his mistress was causing trouble for him at his workplace. It was then that she saw her husband for who he really was - a fallen and weak man.

But he had come to her at last. Even if it was to seek help to clean up his mess. And she had chosen to forgive him. At that point, he was repentant and sincerely apologised. And she also felt like she'd pushed him to it through her obsession with conceiving. Their sex life had become business and mechanical, which wasn't appealing to him. She was also miserable a lot of the time, especially when she got her periods.

But he didn't let her take all the blame. He accepted his fault and promised to be faithful. However, like a pendulum, things swung back to how they had been…because she was still desperate for a child. And this time, she didn't want to bother him about it.

But she never thought he would actually hurt her this way, willingly. She never wanted to find herself in this position again, where she would have to forgive him for a sexual affair. They say, "*fool me once, shame on you... Fool me twice, shame on me...*" What about the third time??? Who is the idiot that hangs around for that?!

Osinachi knew that she was the idiot that would. Even with all he'd done, she still believed that he loved her. He just didn't know how to give her the kind of love she needed. But if he was shown that type of unconditional, selfless, sacrificial, enduring love, he could learn. And she knew that she had to love him that way...as long as God gave her strength. She would show him what real love does.

Osinachi parked her car in the driveway and sat in her car for a couple more minutes. She felt the urge to pray. "Lord, I'm sorry for all the wrong I've done. For being willful and proud. I know You have forgiven me, and that my present suffering is not Your punishment for my disobedience. I believe that Jesus has borne my punishment on the Cross of Calvary, and that when You look at me, You see someone You love and want to bless. I know that my suffering is because of my own wrong choices, and I pray that You will give me wisdom and sincerity of heart to always heed Your counsel going forward.

"Lord, please have mercy on me and on my husband. Lord, please bring him into the knowledge of Your love for him and Your ways. Help me to be a minister to him in my home, to show him the fervent and unrelenting love You show me. Help me not to take his actions personal, but to understand him; to see him through Your eyes, as someone in need of Your grace to do right.

"And Lord, please bless our home. Even though our union was not according to Your will, I know You are a gracious and merciful God, and that Your desire is for all of us to be saved - including Donald. I pray that Your will in his life and in mine will be accomplished in Jesus' mighty name! Amen. Thank You, Lord!"

Osinachi was relieved after that prayer. She felt strengthened as she exited her car to return to her home.

CHAPTER TWELVE

It had been a month since that horrible day, when Mrs Peterson had thrown her out of her home. Only Chinyere knew the hell she had suffered that day before she'd made it to her aunty's place in Abuja. She'd initially thought of going to her Oga's office to let him know what had happened and get some support from him. He worked with a really big multi-national company with their headquarters in Abuja and had previously given her one of their brochures. But when she thought about how she'd fought with his wife, she'd been too ashamed and had doubted that he would help her.

She really wished she had handled it differently. She still didn't know what came over her. She just felt so angry and cheated, and considering her situation, being thrown out without money for transport and food just seemed too wicked.

She'd also been shocked at how easily Oga had lied about what had happened, that night she'd visited them with her aunty. That excuse about her having a boyfriend hadn't even crossed her mind! She'd just thought it was too obvious to deny the truth, and she had never been a good liar. Whenever she thought about how Oga had lied to protect himself, she felt really sad. Angry even. She'd really meant nothing to him... She felt so stupid.

Chinyere had been happy when her aunty had seized the opportunity to demand a bribe from Mr. Peterson. It was the least he deserved. She even wished she had asked for more, because she knew he could afford it! And she wished she had thought of it, rather than her aunty. Now, her aunty acted as if it was her money, and she was doing Chinyere a favour by giving her ten measly percent!

"He was going to give you 30k, two months' salary! If it wasn't for my quick thinking, that's all you'd have - if that!" Aunty Chinwe had said, when she'd insisted that she should keep the bulk of the money.

Chinyere really couldn't complain because her aunty had also given N100,000 to her parents, telling them that it was the compensation Chinyere had received from her former employers. They had been so overjoyed, they hadn't asked more questions about why the couple had suddenly become generous. Also, Aunty Chinwe allowed Chinyere to stay in her apartment and go to school. She had even paid for her school fees from her share of the N1,000,000. So, Chinyere had decided that she was justified to keep the lion share.

They had opened a bank account for Chinyere so that her aunty could transfer the N100,000 to her, which she would save for use at a later date. Previously, Chinyere used to keep N5000 of her wages and send N10,000 home each month. She'd saved up about N20,000 over the months, and used to deposit it in her aunty's account. So, she'd collected her savings from her aunty to open up her new account.

Chinyere was pleased and felt like she was finally in control of her own destiny. She had her own money, and free access to it whenever she wanted. She was going to school and feeding well. Yes, she still cleaned her aunty's apartment, but it was different from when she had worked with Mrs Peterson. This was family, and she was happy to contribute, since she wasn't paying any rent.

Most days, like today, she returned home to cook and clean up the kitchen and bathroom. She would sweep the apartment every morning, before she would have her bath and prepare some breakfast for both of them. Aunty Chinwe usually arrived home before dinner was ready, and the evenings were leisurely.

Chinyere often wondered how Aunty Chinwe could live alone by herself, without a husband or even a boyfriend. Wasn't she lonely? She'd heard from her mother that Aunty had been engaged once before, but no one knew why they never got married...or why he'd left. Chinyere sighed, just as she heard the front door opening. Aunty was back.

***

"Chinyere, when last did you see your period?"

Aunty Chinwe's question came out so unexpectedly during dinner. Chinyere frowned and tried to think. She actually didn't think she had had a period while staying with her aunty. The last one was at Mr. Peterson's house, and that was about a week or two before the incident.

"I can't remember. It has been long..." Then she gasped. "You don't think I'm..." Chinyere gulped. Her first thought was of her education that would be disrupted again.

"You're such a stupid girl!"

"But I was taking the pills..."

"Are you still taking them?"

"No... I'm not having sex."

"When did you stop?"

"That day... When Madam threw me out! She was holding the packet."

Aunty Chinwe shook her head. "You're very stupid. If you had sex with that man, even three days before you stopped, you could still get pregnant."

Chinyere suddenly lost her appetite. "Oh my God! I am pregnant!"

"Thankfully, it is for a stupid, rich and guilty man. We can make profit from this too..." Aunty Chinwe said, smiling wickedly. "If anybody asks who's responsible, tell them you were raped. Gang raped, and you don't know who the father is, okay? He's no use to us in prison."

Chinyere stared at her aunty, horrified by her callousness. Would she even care if her words were fulfilled?

***

"So, it's been about four weeks since your last episode. How are we feeling today?" Dr. Scott asked his patient.

"Fine... Fine," Donald said, with a slight smile.

"That was quite a close call... Have you been able to identify any triggers, yet?"

Donald thought for a while. He knew exactly what had triggered his last psychotic episode, but he wasn't at liberty to disclose it to his psychiatrist. Not then and not now. Not even with their confidential agreement in place. "I just forgot to take my pills that's all. When I forget one, it messes me up, and it's hard to continue taking them," he said, as he shifted in his seat.

"Hmmm..." Dr. Scott muttered, as he jotted something down in his notepad. "I guess that's one of the reasons it's good to have a caregiver. Now that your wife is aware of your condition, that should help you to stay on top of your medications, so that we do not have another re-occurrence."

"Yes, she's been very supportive."

"How does that feel?"

"Great! I'm actually relieved…"

"Hmmm... Why is that?"

"I guess I thought she wouldn't understand."

"Okay... Had she said anything or done anything to make you think that?"

Donald looked down and sighed. "Yes... She used to make fun of mental illness, when we first met."

"Oh... What did she say?"

Donald closed his eyes. "She said that it was a "White

Man's Disease"."

"And what meaning did you draw from that?"

"Basically, she thought it was made up... The way I think her god is made up. She said it's all in our heads, and that poor people don't have time for mental illness, that's why it is only rich nations that have the problem of depression..."

Dr. Scott jotted a few more things down. "Hmmm... So, did that hurt?"

Donald sighed. "I laughed it off, but it did hurt. I found that there was only so much I could tell her, without thinking she would find me weak...or even stupid."

"Okay... Has she said or done anything to make you feel weak and stupid since she found out?"

Donald thought for a while. "No... She's been very gentle and understanding. Maybe, she worries a little too much, and pampers me constantly. She's much more forgiving of my faults." He smiled.

"And how does that make you feel?"

"Loved."

Dr. Scott jotted in his notepad, a small smile on his face.

***

Osinachi had just finished bathing Benjamin, when her phone rang. She swaddled him in a towel and carried him to where she had left her phone. It was her sister, Daluchi. She would have to call her back, when Benjamin was dry, dressed and fed. She wanted to have a good long chat with her, not one that would be interrupted by her divided attention and Benjamin's potential cries.

She hummed as she finished dressing her baby and gave him his feed. She had a new nanny, but she realised that she enjoyed doing these things for her baby. Only when she couldn't get away, she would have the nanny take over. She relied on her nanny to do more of the sterilising of Baby's things and cleaning of the home. Her nanny was her helper, not her replacement, she often told herself, whenever she was feeling lazy.

After he was dressed, fed and happy playing in his playpen, Osinachi left him in the care of his nanny, while she went upstairs to her bedroom to have a chat with her sister. She'd brewed a refreshing cup of tea for the occasion. Just as she was about to call, her phone rang again.

"Hey, Dal! Sorry, I missed your call before..."

"Hi Osi. How are you?"

"I'm good dear. How are you?"

"We're good here. How's Benjamin? And Donald?"

Osinachi sighed happily. "They're both fine... What's going on?"

"Nothing much, dear... I was just thinking it has been three months now since you've had Benjamin. Isn't time for Donald to start adoption procedures?"

Osinachi smacked her hand on her head. "Yeah! Thanks for the reminder. You know, our minds have been on other things..."

"I know... That's why I didn't say anything sooner," Daluchi said. "So, are you guys okay now?"

"Yeah..." Osinachi smiled. "I sometimes think it was too easy... Maybe, I was too stupid, or too weak, or too loving... But, I'm happy! And I know that life is too short to hold on to bitterness."

"That's good. I'm happy for you both. I'm glad that you were *strong* enough to forgive him. Don't ever think it was a weak thing you did. It takes strength to give grace to others."

Osinachi smiled. She needed to hear that. "Thanks, sis."

"How are you coping with his...psychosis?"

"It was hard at first... To see him like that. But it made me realise that we are all so fragile. We are only as strong as our minds, not even our bodies..."

"Yes! You're right. That's why faith is so important."

"Yeah... I admit, we haven't talked much about that since. I've just really been trying to understand him more, and to give him the support he needs. I don't really want to push him beyond what his mind can comprehend."

"Yeah, I get that. Just keep praying for him. And I think it is important for you to expose him to your spirituality. Just as he has exposed you to his *mentality*, he needs to see the practicalities of your faith in God. I think you shouldn't shy away from this and worry that he will reject you. It's like culture... The more we are exposed to it, the more accepting we become of it. So, I hope you will show him your *Christian* culture," Daluchi said, grinning.

"Yes, I will. This has really helped. Thanks, sis!"

"No problem, Osi. We're all praying for you."

"So, how are your kids doing?" Osinachi asked.

Osinachi smiled and laughed as Daluchi told her about her nieces and nephew. With three kids and a husband, Daluchi had a full house. They were not very rich, but they were generous, and they were happy. Daluchi believed in practical Christianity and often opened her home to people in need. It was her big heart that had led her into Nursing, and to her current employment at the General Hospital.

Daluchi often shared heart-breaking stories about people who couldn't afford to pay their hospital bills, or people who had died due to a scarcity of certain drugs. Though she was doing her little bit for humanity by being a nurse and counselling those girls and women whom she came across, who thought they couldn't and shouldn't be burdened to save their child's life, she often thought her little wasn't enough. But her little not only saved those girls' lives, and the lives of their children, it also blessed lives like Osinachi's.

Osinachi smiled as she thought of Benjamin. She was excited about his future. His life mattered, and it was going to count - a great deal!

CHAPTER THIRTEEN

Donald was distracted at the office today. He was thinking about his wife, the beautiful Osinachi. He knew he was lucky to have her. Not only was she beautiful, she was smart. And she was kind and sweet, even though she could be feisty at times. He found her incredibly sexy.

These days, it had been harder for him, because he so wanted to have her again, but though she had forgiven him, she was not yet ready to lie with him. However, they talked and played together. It was like it had been in the beginning, except, this time, she was on lock and key. And it was killing him.

He remembered the night he'd returned from the hospital, how she'd cradled him in her arms, on their bed, and he'd delighted in her ample bosom, rubbing his head on it like a cushion, playfully, and she'd giggled. He'd looked into her eyes then and told her again how sorry he was for cheating on her again. She'd swallowed and kissed him. But when he'd made to prolong the kiss, she'd withdrawn from him.

The next time he'd tried to initiate sex, she'd told him quite plainly that she wouldn't sleep with him until he got tested for everything under the sun! And he'd produced his clean bill of health the next day. He'd actually been nervous because he had been foolish to have sex, with someone other than his wife, without using protection. Chinyere had been a virgin, so he was sure that she was clean. Anyway, he was glad that his test came out clear.

Even with that, she still stopped short of sleeping with him. They made out sometimes, and that was lovely. Wonderful even. But he was desperately in need of a release. And she was the only one he wanted.

Donald sighed, and tried to face his work. Still, he couldn't focus, and was pleased when his PA knocked on his door to report back about some work he had been assigned. After that mess with Gbemi, Donald only hired male secretaries and personal assistants now. Not that he didn't trust himself, but that he didn't think he needed the noose around his neck!

After his PA left with a good report, he felt better about the fact that his day hadn't been all that productive. At least, business was good. He should cut himself some slack. Maybe he could leave early today and take the Mrs out for dinner. The thought was appealing to him. He decided to send her a text message.

***

"*How's your day going?*"

Those four words were as "I love you" to Osinachi. Donald didn't say those three amazing words often, but whenever he sought to communicate with her and find out how she was doing and feeling, and made the effort to show he cared, she now understood loudly and clearly that he was saying he loved her. She was beginning to understand her husband better and appreciate him for just how he was.

Osinachi smiled as she replied his text message. "*It's going good. Thanks. How are things at work?*"

"*It's good too. Though I can't stop thinking of you… When will you be home?*"

Osinachi blushed and beamed at his text. "*By 5pm. Need to*

get some shopping and prepare dinner. Any special requests?"

Donald smiled. "*Dress sexy :)*"

Osinachi's eyes lit up. She grinned. "*Sexy? You mean lingerie?*"

"*I want to take you out... Don't cook tonight. I'll try to get back for 7pm. Is that okay?*"

Osinachi beamed. "*Sounds wonderful! I can't wait :)*"

"*Okay. Cool. Let me get back to work. See you later, Osi.*"

"*Later, babe x.*"

Osinachi smiled. That was a nice and welcome interruption. Donald had been making more effort to connect with her during the day, and also at night these days. Even though things were better between them, she hadn't yet been able to give herself to him again. Not because she didn't want to, but because she ached for a deeper connection, and she didn't want to rush their journey to intimacy again.

The knock on her office door brought her back into the present.

"Come in..." Osinachi said, wistfully.

***

Donald returned home about five minutes to seven that evening. Osinachi was not yet ready. He sat on the sofa and picked up a newspaper from the coffee table to read while he waited.

"I'll be down in a minute!" Osinachi shouted from her dressing room.

She came down about ten minutes later dressed in a red, sleeveless, corset top and dark blue fitted jeans. The corset did wonders for her waistline, and the jeans enhanced her rounded behind. Donald was immediately aroused by the sight of his wife, and now wished he didn't have to sit through a whole meal with her looking so deliciously tempting.

Osinachi was pleased to see that she'd hit the spot with her choice of outfit. She'd been excited at the thought of dressing up for her husband again. His visible response helped to mend her self-esteem, which he had bruised by his betrayal. She thought of making love to him again, and wondered if it would still feel the same... She sighed.

When Osinachi reached his side, Donald took hold of her hand and led her to the door. At the door, he gave in to his desire to kiss his wife fiercely on her lips. His other hand strayed to the curve of her lower back, as he pushed her closer to deepen the kiss. He felt her gasp and open up wider for his tongue to savour her mouth. Oh, his desire for her was so strong.

Donald released his wife eventually, regaining control of himself. He really wanted to take her out and make her feel special. When she looked into his eyes with longing, he stroked her face and said, "That was for looking so damn sexy..."

Osinachi blushed and giggled. She let out a deep sigh as she followed her husband out to his car. It was already promising to be the best night of her life.

***

"Do you remember how we met?"

"How can I forget?" Osinachi smiled. "You were so rude!"

"It wasn't what you thought... I'd really been in the queue before."

"I'd been standing in line for 30 minutes, and I saw you enter the Bank! I can't believe you are still denying that you jumped queue!"

Donald laughed. "Well, the woman in front of you verified my story..."

"Yeah... She probably thought you were going to hit on her or something!" Osinachi hissed.

Donald laughed harder. "Actually, I was... Until you made such a fuss about me jumping the queue..."

"Yeah, I bet you're used to a lot of people turning a blind

eye when you behave so arrogantly. You know they only do that because you're white, right...?"

"It's a gift and a curse," Donald smiled cheekily, and Osinachi rolled her eyes. "Well, I learnt a lesson that day..."

"Oh yeah..."

"You can't always get what you want... Sometimes, you get more," Donald grinned and winked.

Osinachi blushed and shook her head. "You're unbelievable..."

Donald reached out for Osinachi's hands. "I'm still shocked you gave me your number, though..."

"I was just shocked you asked! And you did let me go ahead of you...even though you belonged at least ten spaces behind me!"

Donald giggled. "I thought that was a good sign. You can be firm and principled...but you're very forgiving. We all need someone like that in our lives..."

Osinachi looked at her husband, and then down at their hands clasped together on the dinner table. She was thinking, "*and you're always seeing how much you can get away with*", but decided to keep that thought to herself. He had been self-centred when they'd met. That, strangely, had been part of his appeal. And the fact that he'd wanted her, made her feel honoured and valued in a weird way. She'd felt special...chosen.

"What are you thinking about?" he interrupted her thoughts, using his finger to move some strands of hair from her face.

"Why did you ask me out?"

"Why do men ask women out? You were beautiful..."

"Was that all you saw?"

"I also saw someone that would keep me on my toes... Keep me humble. You were different and I liked you."

Osinachi nodded. "Hmmm... When you didn't call me for weeks, I actually thought maybe you'd bumped into another woman more your type. Or maybe you were just one of those player types, who had a wife or girlfriend that had returned to town on short notice."

Donald smiled. "Actually, I think I was a little afraid of you, if I'm honest. You're not the kind people play with, and I guess I wasn't sure then that I was ready for something serious."

Osinachi smiled. "Yeah... I got that a lot from men. They said I knew what I wanted too much...whatever that means."

"You have a strong mind, and many strong opinions..." Donald released his wife's hand to make room on the table for the waiter to place their order down. When the waiter left, he resumed talking, as he served his plate. "Remember when you said mental illness was a white man's disease?"

Osinachi gasped and covered her open mouth with her hand, as she recalled the conversation. "I did... I'm sorry. Was that why you never told me?"

Donald nodded. "Do you still think that?"

"No... Of course not." Osinachi reached out for her husband. "It was an ignorant thing to say... And I'm sorry I said that. There's a lot I still don't understand about a lot of things... But I know that you weren't faking that day. I was so scared for you."

"You know I wasn't trying to take my life, right? I was unwell... I was also afraid, about the Police getting involved. I just wanted to take my medication and feel better."

"Yes, the doctor said it was probably an accidental overdose," Osinachi said, and swallowed. She was happy to hear Donald confirm it.

Osinachi served herself, and they both ate their food, exchanging looks of understanding and appreciation. She remembered to bring up the issue of adopting Benjamin and was pleased when Donald sounded enthusiastic about it. She asked him if he would still be keen to try for a baby and was once again surprised by his answer.

"I never was keen, Osi. It was what you wanted..."

"But I thought... I thought you wanted a family..."

"Yes... I wanted...I want a family *with you*, because I love you...not because I wanted a family..."

"Oh..."

"And when we couldn't have one, it was okay with me... But I'm happy about Benjamin," Donald smiled. "Will you be content with him, and not worry about having a child of your own?"

Osinachi swallowed. "I've always wanted a daughter. That looked like me and my husband. I've been dreaming of a mixed-raced beauty since we started dating..." she giggled nervously. "Are you saying we are not going to have kids together?"

Donald touched his wife's face gently. "I'm not saying that. We may still have one. I just know that my medical condition could pose a limitation. So, if you're really keen for a girl, we could adopt in a couple of years...if we don't get pregnant."

"Oh... Okay..." Osinachi nodded wearily. "There's so much we didn't say..." She swallowed the lump in her throat, looking downcast.

"Let's not make that mistake anymore. I'm sorry for my part. I just wanted you more than I wanted anything else..."

Osinachi looked up at her husband, and a tear ran down her cheek. She wiped it away. "I'm sorry for my part. I think I wanted you more too. I love you, Donald..."

Donald leaned in and kissed his wife passionately on her lips. "I love you too, Osi."

***

"Oh, Donald! Oh, Donald!" Osinachi cried in bed as her husband pleasured her again. It had been so long. It felt different. It felt better. "Donald!!"

Donald released himself with his final thrust and kissed his wife passionately. She was shaking and sweating in his arms.

She was beautiful, with her eyes closed, writhing in passion. She opened her eyes and he touched her again. She shut them as she gasped with pleasure, arching towards him again.

He kissed her face and pulled her in for a cuddle, when she'd come off her waves of pleasure. He had missed this. Her breathing settled down and, before long, she was asleep in his arms.

"I love you, Osi..." he whispered in the dark.

CHAPTER FOURTEEN

Weeks passed in bliss for the happy couple. Donald completed the paperwork for the adoption of Benjamin, and he was christened Benjamin Idu Peterson. Donald was happy to do the thanksgiving at Osinachi's Church, and his mother came for the occasion.

Osinachi's business began to pick up again, when she finally settled back into a good routine. What helped the most was that she was happy and not mentally distracted with worries. She was also feeling motivated spiritually and had seized the opportunity to talk to Donald about her Faith. He wasn't dismissive like he'd been before, even though he still didn't believe.

Her new nanny was a docile young woman in her twenties. Osinachi had decided that she couldn't live in fear of her husband cheating on her with the help, and so chose someone who she believed was best suited and capable for the job. Amarachi was hardworking and respectful. So far, she had been trustworthy, but Osinachi still didn't know her long enough to leave Benjamin in her care for hours.

She found a Creche that allowed for late pick-ups up till 5pm, at an additional monthly premium. That worked out better for her and enabled her to have a longer day at the office, before going to get her son and returning home to prepare dinner. She liked the owner, who was also a mother with little children. She was sure Benjamin would be happy and safe at the Creche for the longer period, even though few mothers took advantage of this avenue.

Benjamin was four months old now and growing well. Osinachi was watching him as he had tummy time on his play mat in the middle of the sitting room. She rested on Donald, who was reading his newspaper and sipping tea. Amarachi was in the kitchen cleaning up the dishes they had used for dinner. Another fifteen minutes and she'd get Benjamin tucked in for the night, Osinachi thought lazily.

The doorbell interrupted their perfect moment. Amarachi went to answer it.

"Ma, Ibrahim say two women de for gate... He wan know if they fit enter," Amarachi spoke in broken English.

"Two women?" Osinachi asked. "They no get names?"

"He no tell me, oh. Make I ask..."

"I'm coming..." Osinachi rose up and slipped on her slippers. Ibrahim was at the door. "Who are they?"

"Na Chinyere and her aunty, Madam. Se they fit enter?"

Osinachi was puzzled. Them again? She looked at the time on her watch. It was 8:30pm. She didn't want to disrupt her home, so she decided to follow Ibrahim to the gate. What could they be after this time?

When she stepped out of the gate, she looked at Chinyere first, and then her aunty. Instinctively, her eyes returned to what looked like a rise on the girl's belly. She already knew why they came, and she dared not query them at the gate.

Her heart raced as she said, "Come in."

***

It was her day off, and Daluchi was outside in her backyard, tending to her tomato garden. It was both a hobby and another source of livelihood for her family. After reaping their harvest of tomatoes, they often had enough to trade at the local market. She had trained all her children to love and tend the garden, and on how to preserve them too.

She carried a bucket of ripened tomatoes to process in her kitchen and turned to return to her house, when she saw the unexpected visitor. Daluchi paused as she looked at the young girl, surprised and unsure of how to respond to her visit. She suspected it wasn't for good news.

"Sorry, aunty. I would have called," the girl said. "But…"

Daluchi frowned at the girl. "Are you okay?"

"Yes, ma. I am. Please, I want to speak with you."

"Sure, come in," Daluchi said, leading the way into the house, through the kitchen.

She dropped her produce on the kitchen counter and opened the fridge to get a cold jug of water, which she carried with her to the living room with a glass cup. She set them on a coffee table and motioned for Uloma to take a seat, while pouring the girl a drink. The girl sat down nervously. Daluchi thought she looked better, healthy. She sighed.

"So, why have you come back?"

"Ma, I want to say thank you for everything you did for me. You really saved my life. I was so miserable then that I thought I would die, but you gave me hope. Thank you, ma."

Daluchi took in a deep breath and smiled. Few of those she helped ever came back to say thanks. But she wasn't in the habit of bringing them to stay at her home. She'd made this exception because the child was for her sister. Otherwise, Uloma would not have known where she lived.

"You're welcome," she said, tentatively, knowing there was more to the visit.

"But ma… I've changed my mind. I want my baby."

Daluchi closed her eyes, because she had known that was the reason the moment she saw the girl. She slowly shook her head. "I'm sorry, dear. But it's too late."

Uloma's eyes opened wide in shock and unbelief. "But he's my son!"

"And you signed your parental rights away. He is no longer your son, and you can't ask for him back. It's not fair."

Uloma swallowed, as her eyes pooled with hot tears. She sniffled. "Aunty, please. I want my baby! I made a mistake."

Daluchi sighed. She always gave them a good talk about their options and the decision they were making, before and during the whole process. But it wasn't uncommon for some to return to request their babies back. In these few cases, she was always adamant that it couldn't be done.

Usually, the legal process was completed with both birth parents signing off their rights, and she never ever went back to the adoptive parents to request for the reversal of the adoption process. Apart from it being unfair to them, it wasn't often in the best interest of the child, who was already stable in their home environment. But this case was different and she knew it. Still, she didn't want to give the girl any idea that she would be successful in her campaign to reverse the adoption process.

"I'm sorry, I can't help you with that. It is not fair on the new parents nor the child."

Uloma sat crying. "I know you know the aunty that took my baby. I know you can help me. If you speak to her…"

Daluchi just shook her head. "I'm really sorry you feel this way." She wanted to add "*I wish there was something I could do*", but she realized that it wasn't the truth. There was something she could do. She could ask Osinachi. But she didn't want to. Her sister would be inconsolable if she lost Benjamin now. "I did tell you this before we started the process, and even before you signed the papers. I told you that you can't reverse your decision. And if you change your mind, you'd have to go to court…" She thought it was only fair to the girl to add that bit about her legal right to pursue the case in court.

Uloma wiped her eyes and straightened her expression. "I

will go to court. I know I have rights. The father doesn't know about the baby, but I will tell him, and he will fight for his child!"

"*What?!*" Daluchi said, alarmed. "But you said…"

Uloma smiled. "Andrew was not the father. He thought he was, but he wasn't. The father is in my hometown in Enugu. And I will tell him. And we will come for our baby!"

Daluchi just stared at the girl before her, unable to believe her eyes and ears. This was such a minefield, trying to help others. Sometimes, you get burned.

***

Osinachi was in her office when Daluchi's call came through. "Hey."

"Hey, Osi. How are you?"

Osinachi breathed out a deep sigh. She was so stressed. By work, by motherhood and by the news she'd received last night. Daluchi was just the person she needed to talk to. "Not good right now. I actually wanted to call you later."

"Why? What's up?" Daluchi asked, putting her update aside.

"Chinyere's pregnant."

"Huh? Who's…"

"My house help. The girl that used to work for us… She's carrying my husband's baby," Osinachi said with a sob. "She came last night… God, I don't even know what to do or how to feel or anything. I just feel…numb."

"Oh, Osinachi. I'm so sorry!" Daluchi said. "How is Donald? How was he?"

"He's sorry. What more can he do at this point? They made some demands for her upkeep and medical fees, and we agreed."

"Hmmm…"

"I'm worried for the girl, though. That her aunty is something else. I've never seen anyone so greedy in my life!"

"Really? Well, what can you do about it? Just be glad that

they aren't taking legal action against you... You know, even having an under-aged house help is a criminal offence."

"Yeah... Thank God," Osinachi breathed out a sigh of relief.

"Speaking of legal action... Uloma came to see me."

Osinachi sat up straight on her executive chair. "Yeah...? What about?"

"She wants Benjamin back. But I told her it's too late."

"She can't take him back, nau... We've completed the paperwork and everything! Thank God for that!"

"Well, actually... There might be a problem."

"Huh? What do you mean?"

"Well, we assumed the father wasn't interested in the baby, based on her story. But she's now saying the father didn't even know about the baby and would be interested once she tells him!"

"Oh my God! But she's lying! I'm sure she's lying again..."

"Probably, but... We have to be ready in case she isn't," Daluchi said. "If they demand a paternity test, and it is proven that this other guy is the father, they can take us to court to get their baby back."

"Their baby?! It's my baby, Daluchi! They were not married and he wasn't interested, and we did everything right," Osinachi said, feeling like she was losing it. Why was all this happening to her?

"Not knowing is different from not being interested. The father has rights too," Daluchi said. "Look dear, I'm really sorry about everything you've been going through. But God is in control. Don't forget that, okay? I just wanted you to consider it, and get back to me, after discussing with Donald, whether or not you will be going to court or giving up Benjamin willingly..."

Osinachi wiped her tears with the back of her hand. "What do you think we should do?"

"Honestly, Osinachi, if Benjamin was older, I would fight. But he's still very young, and I think if there's a chance his birth parents want him back, and they are even willing to go to court over it, then you should probably give him up. I know you really want to be a mother, but Uloma was and has realised that she still wants to be. But don't listen to me. Pray and discuss with your husband, okay?"

"Okay. I'll talk to him. Thanks, Dal."

"I'm sorry. I didn't want this to break down. I feel partly to blame."

"Daluchi, you did nothing wrong! You've been an angel, but you're not God, okay? I'll be fine. Thanks!"

"Thanks, Osinachi. Sometimes, I forget I can only do so much. Talk later."

Osinachi sighed deeply after ending the call. Was this another case of "man plans, but the Lord decides"?! She knew she hadn't pursued this adoption in the right way or even with a right spirit. But was she wrong to desire a child so much? And it seemed so unfair that her husband could father a child with her maid and not with her. She held her face in her hands and cried. *Father, I know it's not Your intention, but this hurts so bad!*

***

Osinachi told Donald about Benjamin's birth mother that night, over dinner. He was devastated for her.

"I'm so sorry, Osinachi! I really am," he said. "But I don't think we can fight it…"

She knew what he meant. That was all she had been thinking about all day. Given his history with Chinyere, and her pregnancy, they really didn't need any official attention into their lives. She nodded in understanding.

"I think we can still see if we could adopt Chinyere's baby, though."

Osinachi eyed her husband. She remembered how rude the girl and her aunty had been when she'd initially suggested it. She was just trying to let them know how supportive they were willing to be. She wasn't really keen on having a constant reminder of her husband's betrayal and her inability to conceive or carry to term. She swallowed.

"I mean, seeing as I'm the biological father, there is no one to contest the adoption. That's if she agrees, of course. If we really want a child, it's worth another try…"

Osinachi sighed and nodded. If that was all the grace she would be given, she would accept it with humility. "Yeah, I guess."

She tried to smile, and Donald took her hand to kiss it. "Thank you," he said, with an appreciative smile.

CHAPTER FIFTEEN

Osinachi and Donald journeyed down to Lagos together to hand Benjamin over to his birth mother. Donald thought it was important that he show his support to his wife by going along. He was also going to miss the baby boy he had come to know as his son.

The mother of the child looked no older than eighteen years old, and for a moment, Donald wished that he could have challenged her plea, seeing as she looked as though she was struggling to look after her own self. Osinachi had been stoic right up to the point she handed the baby to Daluchi, who then passed him on to his birth mother. And then she broke down in sobs in his arms.

"Thank you, aunty," Uloma said sincerely. "I'm sorry," she added, as she rose up from her seat and tied a crying Benjamin to her back with a cloth wrapper.

It was the cries of Benjamin that got to Donald, and he didn't know when he too started to sob. Daluchi escorted the girl out of her home, and put her into a cab, though the girl said she would be alright with public transportation. For Daluchi, that was her last due diligence, as she didn't want anything happening to the baby as he left her care. She prepared and brought tea and cookies, which she had baked earlier for the occasion, and placed them on the coffee table for the grieving couple.

Donald pulled himself together first, as he soothed his wife with comforting words. "It's going to be okay, Osinachi. Benji is going to be fine. Just be glad that you were part of giving him a chance and you gave him a good start in life. If not for you, his story could have been so different. You've done your part, honey. And we can try again…"

Osinachi sniffled. She didn't want to be comforted and told that she could replace Benjamin. She'd loved him like her own; like she had carried him for nine months and birthed him herself. She had plans for him, for them. *Oh, God, why???*

"But what if it happens again?! If this can happen, what's the guarantee that we can ever have a secure adoption?" she asked, looking between her husband and her sister, who both returned her gaze with empathy.

"Honestly, Osinachi, we will just have to be more selective and diligent in ensuring that every loophole is covered. So, some cases like this with a single girl or woman, we will just have to give a miss, because there's only so much we can do to verify their stories. We would need to confirm paternity and also ensure that the father knows about and supports the adoption process. That's really all you can do to be safe, dear. And we can keep praying for a miracle," she added, looking at the pair.

Donald nodded, to show his support and understanding, even though he didn't believe nor agree that more prayer would change anything. Osinachi had been praying for years, and there was no evidence that God either existed, could hear or even cared about her prayer. But he didn't want to voice his negative thoughts to Osinachi, who needed encouragement and hope right now.

"But do you think by trying to adopt a child, we are helping God?" Osinachi asked, remembering the sermon she'd listened to in Church a month or so ago.

Donald thought that was an interesting question, and actually illustrated one of his problems with "faith". He thought it was stupid that people would reject doing the things that would get them what they wanted, because they were waiting on a "miracle" from a "supreme being". Especially in a country with as many issues as Nigeria, religion seemed to be the cover for all sorts of negligence and incompetence, and he found it objectional. Still, he waited to see how Daluchi would respond.

"No dear, I don't think that's always the case… It depends on your revelation from and relationship with God. Have you sought God's face about going the adoption route?" Daluchi asked.

Donald put his head in his hand to keep from rolling his eyes. *Seriously?! You have to ask permission from God to adopt a baby?!*

Osinachi shook her head. "No… I didn't before."

"Well, that's important. Adopting a child, as you have seen, is an important decision for you, the child and the mother. If marriage requires seeking God's face to enter with wisdom, how much more so adopting and raising a child?" Daluchi asked.

"But is it wrong to adopt?"

"No, it isn't wrong. It's a really good avenue for a lot of people and helps a lot of vulnerable women and girls. But, like I said before, what has God told you?" Daluchi asked. When Osinachi remained unsure, she wondered how she could make her point clearer. "You know, the story of Abraham and Sarah, right? God promised them a child, but the promise was delayed. And Sarah, who didn't have faith, offered her maid to Abraham, and he agreed to father a child with the maid, but that wasn't the child of promise. Do you remember how things turned out?"

Osinachi nodded. "The maid became resentful and Sarah

became jealous and eventually asked her to leave with the child."

"Yeah... And even beyond that, when she did have the promised child, eventually, in God's good time, the first child of the flesh became a thorn to the Israelites, the children of promise. Yet, God had mercy on the maid and her child, and his children. He still blessed them, even though they were not conceived by His will, but came about as a result of disobedience. We have to make sure that we are walking in faith and obedience if we want God's best."

Osinachi wiped her tears. It was the same sermon again. She realised that her problem was a lack of faith in God. Not so much in His ability, but in His graciousness to bless her and answer her prayer. She was still developing her ability to listen and hear from God, and part of the problem was her own impatience and willfulness. She knew if she heard God say "No" to her request, it would break her heart, and she couldn't bare to hear His objection to this great desire of her heart.

As if hearing her thoughts, Daluchi added, "God is a good God, and He delights in giving good gifts to His children, Osinachi. Don't be afraid to ask God for what you really want. Just be humble enough to accept His will and to obey. And if you dare, you can be like the persistent widow. Jesus said that if we persist in prayer, God will eventually answer us."

"So, which one are we praying for...? Permission to adopt, or for God to give us a child of our own?" Donald decided to ask, feeling a little confused about the discussion.

"Well, we can do both. And He may answer both at once or close the door to one and open the other. The point is we surrender our will to Him and show our faith by trusting Him to lead us," Daluchi said, smiling warmly at him. She was pleased that he was part of their discussion today.

"Thanks, sis," Osinachi said. "I think this baby, or the idea of having a baby, has been an idol in my heart I have placed above God. And I think it has actually hindered me from seeing God for what He really is, my great reward, and chasing after Him as I should. I'm going to forsake it and focus on God. If I get pregnant, then glory be to God. And if not, He knows best."

Daluchi stood up then and went to hug her sister, with tears in her eyes. "He is your great reward and He knows best. God, thank You for helping Osinachi to see that You are God and God alone. I pray that as she puts this desire and burden down, You will show her what great plans You have for her, and fill her with a passion to do Your will." Reaching out to hold Donald's hand, she added, "Thank You for Donald too. Please bless their marriage and make them fruitful to the glory of Your name alone, amen."

"Amen," Osinachi said, hugging her sister back and breathing out a deep sigh.

Donald wasn't sure, but there was something electric about Daluchi's touch. He cradled his left hand, which she had held moments ago, in his right, as he pondered on it, and on her prayer point. For his wife's sake, he said, "Amen."

***

The months passed by, and Osinachi grew in her relationship with God. She no longer lived with a hole in her heart for a baby, but rather a hole in her heart to know God more. She was like the deer that pants for the water, as she sought Him in prayer, meditation and fellowship. She also realised, through volunteering with a charity she had only previously donated to, that in service to others and in simplicity, there was so much more joy to be found in life.

Osinachi also took more interest in Donald and his care needs. She learnt about the foods that he preferred to eat, and also incorporated more healthy meals into their diet. The difference was clear in how much better Donald ate and slept, and in his general countenance throughout the day. He was less stressed and more energized, motivated and focused.

He had been a bit of a fitness freak when they had married and had tried to rope her into doing exercises with him, but she never saw the need in it. She didn't want to be bothered about exercising, especially as she was naturally slender, and loved her curves. Overtime, he had lost his motivation and diligence in it, and it was showing in his weight and general energy levels.

It was after her discovery of his mental health condition that she realised why he had been so eager to exercise earlier. Among the few side effects of his medication was weight gain. And even though she didn't mind, he was self-conscious about it.

So, she now joined him to do his exercises, to encourage him to stay motivated and fit. And the difference was clear as day. Not only was he happier and fitter, he was also more easily aroused by her and performed better in bed. And if that wasn't enough benefit, her decision to and the time they spent working out together deepened their bond so much that their love grew stronger. And she was very happy.

Osinachi sang as she prepared the salad for their Sunday brunch. It was an old worship song she'd often heard her mother singing; "Take My Life And Let It Be" written by Frances Havergal. She liked to sing it to herself often these days, to remember her decision to surrender all to God and to live for Him.

Since they returned from handing Benjamin over, she hadn't revisited the issue of adoption. It still wasn't easy seeing other women pregnant, but she was done comparing her life to others. She had lots to be thankful and hopeful for. For one, Donald had been asking her more questions about her Faith, and they'd been having pretty interesting discussions. She was optimistic that he would soon see the light.

Osinachi brought the bowl of salad to complete the table

she had decorated and called to her husband to come down for brunch. She watched him as he came down the stairs, admiring him anew. He was really a handsome man and even sexier now that he was fitter. She sighed deeply and averted her eyes when he returned her gaze.

"You're checking me out again, aren't you?" he teased.

She hissed, playfully. "You're too full of yourself, Mr. Peterson!"

He laughed out loud. He leaned towards her and gave her a passionate kiss on her lips. "You're too shy to confess what you want, my love…"

Osinachi thought that was a strange thing for him to say but decided not to dwell on it. They sat down and she prayed over the food, holding his hand to include him. And afterwards, they both said "Amen" in unison. She smiled at how he didn't seem to mind her new practice of praying with him.

"Hmmm… Delicious," he muttered, as he took a spoonful of the baby prawns in tomato sauce she'd made with the help of a cookbook. Osinachi smiled proudly. "So… We haven't talked about this in a while, but Chinyere should be half-way through her pregnancy by now."

Osinachi chewed on her mouthful as she looked at her husband, wondering where he was going with his observation. "Hmmm hmm."

"I think we should revisit the idea of adoption," he said, looking at her pointedly.

"But…"

"I know you've forsaken the idea… But, I'm kinda keen to have a little one in our family. And I know it would make you happy… I think we should approach them again."

Osinachi swallowed. She hadn't heard anything from God on the matter, and she didn't want to do anything that wouldn't bear good fruit in her life. Was this really God's will or just the whim of a man in love? *Listen to him.* Osinachi paused for a minute. Had she heard correctly?

"Are you okay?" Donald asked. Osinachi looked distracted.

"Ummm, yeah. I thought I heard something…"

Donald frowned, not knowing what she meant. "Well, why don't you pay Chinyere another visit, sometime this week? It wouldn't hurt, would it?"

Go, Osinachi. Osinachi swallowed because she was sure now that God was ministering to her through her husband. "Sure…" she said, as hope and joy crept into her heart, widening her lips with a smile.

CHAPTER SIXTEEN

January 2004. Kuje District, Abuja.

Chinyere was depressed. Her life was not her own. She felt so out of touch with what was happening to her...and in her body. The unwanted intrusion that was a life growing within, which she had no power to terminate. That right had been taken from her. The choice was a political decision she could not afford to make.

She felt so badly cheated. Not only by the man who was responsible for her current predicament, but by the woman who was taking advantage of her. Who used her as a bargaining chip to extort another, not even considering her feelings and wishes.

When she considered the world, Chinyere felt so miserable. So lonely and alone. There was no one she could talk to. No one to confide in. No one to understand nor help her.

She now wished she had not followed her aunty to Abuja, nor agreed to work for the Petersons. None of their promises had come to fruition. She was still uneducated, while her mates were sitting exams to attend higher educational institutions. She couldn't even concentrate on reading these days. She was constantly tired and uncomfortable. She was irritable and angry. She was just frustrated!

She wished she could run away from it all. She wished the baby would die and leave her alone. She wished she had never given in to her lust and given herself to Mr. Peterson. She hated herself for being so foolish. And she hated him for being so weak!

The night she had told the Petersons of her pregnancy, she hadn't known what to expect. She definitely hadn't expected that they would offer to adopt the child! She'd been relieved and angry at the same time. Relieved because she saw that she had options... And angry because they had been presumptuous!

What right did they have to deny her of her child?! Just because they had money, did they think they could buy her child?! Even if she wanted to put the baby up for adoption, it certainly wouldn't be to that wicked couple!

Aunty Chinwe had also rejected the notion of adoption. The child was theirs, she'd said. The child was family, and their family would take care of their own. All she wanted from the Petersons was for them to take responsibility for the pregnancy, pay for Chinyere's medical fees and personal care until the child's birth, and pay child support after the baby is born. The Petersons had agreed to Aunty Chinwe's terms, and even apologised for their actions, which had been surprising to Chinyere.

It had been three months since, and Chinyere was on her 21st week. The Petersons sent N250,000 monthly to Aunty Chinwe for medical expenses and Chinyere's upkeep. Chinyere knew they spent nowhere near that amount each month. She got N50,000 from her aunty monthly, which she used on herself, or saved up. She mostly saved the money, as she intended to leave her aunty, and find a place to stay by herself, once she had delivered her baby. Her aunty could keep or sell the baby for all she cared!

Aunty Chinwe lived better these days. She bought new things in her apartment that had nothing to do with Chinyere nor childcare. She bought new clothes and jewellery and went out a lot. Chinyere hated her.

Chinyere refused to do any more housework, apart from washing dishes occasionally. Aunty Chinwe got someone else to clean, as she tried to maintain a higher standard of living, and also appease the source of her new-found fortune. She also had a new boyfriend, who visited her during the weekends. Chinyere would hear them having sex in the middle of the day and think what a couple of idiots they were. She couldn't wait to leave that house!

***

Chinyere was surprised one day to receive a visit from Osinachi. Since the last visit she'd made with her aunty to the Petersons, she hadn't heard from either of them. Aunty Chinwe related to them concerning all her needs. And Chinyere had been happy not to have any direct contact with the couple. She was nervous today to welcome Osinachi into her home, especially since her aunty was away at work.

"Hi Chinyere," Osinachi greeted. She was holding a bowl with sweet smelling food. "Can I come in?"

"What is it?" Chinyere replied, irritably. She didn't trust this woman.

"I just wanted to check on how you are doing... And I brought you some lunch," Osinachi replied with a smile.

Chinyere wasn't sure. She thought for a moment, looked about anxiously, and considered the gift of food before saying "Okay, thanks."

Osinachi walked in to the small two-bedroom apartment. She placed her dish on the dining table and stood awkwardly until Chinyere offered her a seat. "Thanks."

Chinyere went into the kitchen to get a plate and a spoon. She had just been about to make herself some two-minute noodles, so this was a pleasant alternative. She opened the bowl to find freshly cooked jollof rice, grilled chicken, fried plantain, moi-moi and salad. It was a feast! Her mouth watered as she served herself, wondering if she should offer her guest. She decided it wasn't necessary.

"So, how are you doing?" Osinachi asked, when Chinyere returned with a tray to eat in the living room.

"I'm fine," Chinyere said, dropping the "Ma" that was at the tip of her tongue. The woman was not worthy of that respect, she told herself.

"How far gone are you now?"

"Five months."

Osinachi nodded. "Do you know the sex?"

"It's a girl..."

"Oh, wow! You're growing well," Osinachi beamed. She looked about the house. It was clean and tidy. She was pleased to see that Chinyere was being well looked after. "When's your next appointment?"

"Why?"

"I thought it would be nice to come with you. Would that be okay?"

"My aunty will be there," Chinyere lied. Her aunty never accompanied her for her doctor's visits. And she was still attending the local hospital, not the private ones that cost more money. "You don't have to."

"I know... But, I'd still like to. You know... The baby's my family too."

Chinyere looked up at Osinachi, annoyed. "You do not have the right! After what you people did to me, you cannot tell me that this baby is your child!"

Osinachi expected this, so she didn't react. She swallowed. "You can't say we don't have the right, while you expect us to provide for the child as though it is ours. It is only because we believe that the child in your womb is my husband's seed that we are being so generous... If she is not our family, you wouldn't have any right to our support. It's a two-way thing, Chinyere."

"It is only because you do not want to go to prison! You should thank me for not reporting you!"

"Do you know that it is a crime to offer a bribe? To obstruct justice? That's what you and your aunty did when you demanded a million naira from my husband. You cannot keep using that against us! We are sorry for what happened to you while you were in our home. But this baby is not a bargaining chip you can use for the rest of your life! If you do not want the baby... If you do not love this baby, we do, and we are ready and *able* to look after it. That's the reason we are giving you as much support as you need."

Chinyere swallowed. "So, you really want to adopt my baby?"

"Yes, we do. If you are happy to look after it alone, that's okay and we will continue to support you. But please, don't deny us from being a part of the child's life..."

"Okay. I'll think about it."

Osinachi smiled. "Thank you." She swallowed nervously. "Can I ask one more thing?"

Chinyere looked up suspiciously, preparing herself to say "No". "What?"

"Can I touch your tummy?" Chinyere's eyebrows shot up. "I want to feel the baby kicking..."

Slowly, Chinyere smiled. Her aunty had never shown any interest in the baby nor how she was dealing with the pregnancy. She was really surprised that Mrs Peterson would make such a request. She nodded and giggled when Osinachi touched her rounded stomach and the baby gave two kicks.

***

Chinyere was now in her ninth month of pregnancy. She was full, heavy and glowing. Her last trimester had been much better than the first two, owing to the improved relationship she had with Osinachi and Donald, who she finally allowed to begin procedures for the adoption of her baby, despite opposition from her aunty.

She became a regular visitor at the Petersons' home, where she was welcomed and treated to ice-cream, cakes and anything she craved. She also resumed her tutoring sessions, to keep up with her studies, especially as she had nothing but time on her hands. She was chauffeur-driven home by their driver whenever she visited, and her taxi fares to visit the Petersons were always settled by Mrs Peterson. Mrs Peterson also registered Chinyere at their family hospital and attended the doctor's appointments with her.

Though Chinyere was happy about these changes, she still had a nagging worry. She'd tried not to think of it much earlier in her pregnancy, especially as she was still very mad about being pregnant in the first place and being used as a pawn for profit by her aunty. But now that her relationship with the Petersons was better, and now that she neared her delivery date, she was more and more anxious about her dilemma. She really hoped that it would be a needless worry. She prayed that everything would happen as planned and expected.

Still, she wondered how things would change once the baby came. Would they adopt the baby and want nothing more to do with her? Would they still be nice and supportive towards her? What if she changed her mind about the adoption? What if all this love was only conditional on her giving them her baby and not pressing charges on Mr. Peterson's assault?

Chinyere closed her eyes and shivered slightly. There was no use worrying. Everything was going to be fine. She would have her baby, and she would move out of her aunty's place. In September, she would resume school and her life would be back on track. *In Jesus' name, amen!*

"Are you cold?" Osinachi asked, looking worriedly at Chinyere, who sat on the sofa licking ice-cream. She knew the girl could deliver any day now and wished she would accept her offer to spend the night. She really didn't want anything to complicate the birth of her daughter.

Chinyere looked up and smiled at Osinachi. She shook her head. "No, I think it's the ice-cream."

"Let me turn down the AC, so you're comfortable."

"No, please. I like it cool. Thanks, Ma."

Osinachi smiled and then went to the kitchen. She returned with some fruit she had sliced, just as Chinyere was getting up. "Everything okay?"

"I need to pee..."

Osinachi dropped the bowl of fruit and hastened to assist Chinyere from the sofa, even though she knew she could manage. It was just in time too, as Chinyere's water broke when she rose up completely from her seat. The ladies turned to look at each other, one smiling and the other in shock.

Osinachi assisted Chinyere to her car, before rushing back into the house to get her handbag and another bag of essentials she had prepared. She quickly called Donald to alert him of the baby's arrival. He said he would meet them at the hospital. She also called Ms. Ebuka when they got to the hospital. She said she would come as soon as she could. Osinachi checked Chinyere into a private room for the delivery, and sat waiting, while the nurses attended to her.

Donald arrived about 20 minutes after they were settled in. Ms. Ebuka came an hour later. However, when the consultant arrived, they were all asked to leave the room, except for the father of the child. Chinyere asked Osinachi to stay with her, while the others waited outside.

"You're nicely dilated now..." the consultant gynaecologist said, after performing the umpteenth check. "I need you to take in some deep breaths, and push when I tell you to, okay?"

Chinyere nodded. She was sweating, and Osinachi went to

her side and dabbed her face with a napkin. She held her hand, and Chinyere squeezed it tight as she pushed through a big contraction.

"I can see the baby's head... You're doing good! Keep pushing!"

Suddenly, the room was filled with the cry of a new-born baby. Osinachi was so happy. She watched in anticipation as the baby was revealed. Her expression changed and she swallowed and blinked rapidly, unable to believe her eyes. She turned to the mother of the child, as the baby was taken away to be cleaned.

The girl's eyes were wide with shock, and she began to cry.

CHAPTER SEVENTEEN

Donald and Ms. Ebuka were let back into the room, when the baby was delivered. Chinyere was still crying and hadn't been able to say anything. Osinachi was sitting down on a visitor's chair looking very confused.

"Hey, what's going on?! Is the baby okay?" Donald asked, anxiously.

"Yes, we heard the beautiful cry! Why are you crying, Chinyere?" Ms. Ebuka asked her niece.

"The baby is black," Osinachi almost whispered to Donald.

"What do you mean by "black"? Her mother is African..."

"No, Donald. She's full African! Dark-skinned black. She's not mixed-raced! She's not yours!"

Donald looked at Chinyere, confused. Ms. Ebuka looked at the couple, thinking this must be some joke. She was about to challenge Osinachi when the nurse returned with the baby, and she saw there was no way that child could be Donald's!

"Chinyere... What is this about? Whose baby is this??!" Ms. Ebuka exclaimed.

Chinyere just sobbed, while everyone watched her and waited for her response. Nobody expected to hear her say "I don't know..."

Ms. Ebuka put her hand on her head and started wailing dramatically. "Hey oh! Chineke! God oh! See me see trouble, oh! Which kind pikin be this sef?! Oh, Chinyere!"

"Chinyere, what do you mean you don't know?" Donald asked. This was alarming to him. He felt cheated! He really had no idea who he had been sleeping with.

Chinyere looked at the nurse, nervously, and Osinachi took the baby from her and asked her to leave them. "Chinyere, please, we need an explanation for this... Who else were you sleeping with?" she asked, as she placed the baby down in its crib.

"Ibrahim..."

"Our former security guard, *Ibrahim???*" Osinachi asked in disbelief. She now remembered that he had absconded the weekend after Chinyere had visited to announce her pregnancy.

Chinyere nodded. Donald sat down suddenly in shock.

"What is the matter with you?! What were you doing sleeping with the security?!" Ms. Ebuka asked, accusingly.

"He find out about me and Oga and say he go report to Madam if I no gree for him too..." Chinyere said, feeling sick just thinking about it.

"Oh my God! How long was that going on for?" Osinachi asked.

"About a month..." she swallowed.

Donald shook his head with regret. Because of what he did, someone else decided to take advantage of the poor girl. This was terrible! And he had thought his act was harmless to her.

"So, it is his baby then...?" Osinachi asked.

"She said she doesn't know! That means there was someone else!" Ms. Ebuka said in a raised voice.

Chinyere held her face in her hands. She really wished she didn't have to recount this horrible incident. If the baby had been Donald's maybe she could have pretended that it never happened. She was, however, too emotional and tired to try to speak in proper English and grammatical accuracy, so she relied on broken English, which she spoke fluently.

"The day wey you throw me commot for house," Chinyere began, looking at Osinachi. "I think say I go go my aunty office, but the place dey far. I don tire for sun and I begin dey stop taxi for road. I tell them say make they drop me for Federal Secretariat, that I no get money, but I go settle for dere when I con see my aunty, but they no gree for me. Na so one policeman con waka come meet me. Him think se na ashawo work I dey do…

"I tell am say na my Madam wey throw me commot for house, after she don beat me. He still dey talk say make I follow am go station to report the matter. I tell am say I no wan report anything, I just wan go see my aunty for Secretariat. I say I just wan beg money for transport, but he talk say I must follow am go station.

"So, I con follow am go Station. I don dey sit dere tay…time don go. I think say make I ask the Madam wey dey take report. I con tell am say I don wait tire, but I no wan report anything, and I never see the policeman wey carry me come again. Na money I dey find to take go my aunty place. She ask if I dey sell body for road, and I tell am say I no dey do ashawo work, oh. Na so she con let me go. But I still never see the policeman wey carry me go again."

"Mtcheew!" Ms. Ebuka hissed. "He probably thought you would sleep with him so he would let you go… Useless idiot!"

"The time wey I leave police station, e don dark small. I don dey feel like say person dey follow me for back. I still never get money for transport, and I don dey fear to stop moto again. Time don reach to go aunty office, so I don dey trek go her house. 30 minutes don pass and I don tire, so I stop for one corner, make I rest. Na so one man drag me commot and rape me for side of building."

Osinachi dropped to her knees in tears. "Oh, God! Oh, God! Oh, God!"

"When the first one don finish, him friend enter me again, before the third one con come... Na three of them dey dere."

"No!!!" Donald cried aloud, cradling his head in his hands as he sobbed. If he hadn't done what he did, she wouldn't have been in that situation. Ibrahim wouldn't have blackmailed her. She would be in school now, instead of being a drop-out, teenage mother, alone without a clue who the father of her baby is! It was all his fault, Donald thought, as he sobbed.

"So, how did you get to my apartment?" Ms. Ebuka asked, sounding a little doubtful.

"One taxi man con see wetin dem dey do and begin press horn. The men don dey run, and he con carry me go General Hospital. He give me small money wey I fit use take buy medicine. When he con go, I no enter hospital again. I con enter another moto and give am your address."

The room fell silent. The question was hanging in the air: who would take responsibility for this baby? Would Chinyere be left alone to look after it? Would the Petersons conclude the process of adoption they'd already began? Would her aunty and family stand with her to care for the child?

Ms. Ebuka was thinking of all the money she would no longer be getting for child support. She was thinking of the new business she would have to pull out of, now that her fortunes had changed. She was worried that she would be asked to return money she'd already spent. She was thinking of the cost of looking after Chinyere and her new baby, without its rich sponsors. And without a word, she slipped out of the hospital room.

***

After her aunty left, Chinyere turned to her side, grieved and expectant of more rejection. Sad tears rolled down her cheeks. What was she going to do now? She closed her eyes and wished Mr. and Mrs Peterson would just leave now, instead of prolonging whatever this was. She wanted to spare them the guilt and tell them it was okay for them to go too, but when she opened her mouth to speak, she croaked a cry instead.

Donald called his wife aside, and they went to a corner of the room briefly. Chinyere could hear them whispering but couldn't discern what they were saying. Then she felt a hand on her shoulder. She turned to see Donald and Osinachi looking at her, both teary eyed.

"Chinyere, I am so ashamed of what I did to you...taking advantage of you the way I did. I was horribly selfish and wicked. I hate what I exposed you to, and the things you suffered because of my actions. I can't help but feel responsible for everything you went through in my house and since. There's nothing I can do to make it alright. All I can do is plead your forgiveness. Please forgive me!" Donald said, as he got on his knees.

Chinyere looked at him, and then up at the ceiling. She didn't know how to feel about his apology, in light of her current predicament. Osinachi got on her knees too.

"Chinyere, I was so hurt and angry when I found out about you two. But I was wrong to beat you. I was wrong to throw you out helplessly from my house. For a crazy moment, I forgot that you were just a child in my care, entrusted to my protection and training. I was the one who let you down. I'm sorry for all that I failed to do, and what I refused to see because I was too concerned about me. Please forgive me!"

Tears rolled freely down Chinyere's cheeks. She was touched by their apologies, especially Osinachi's admittance of neglect and physical abuse. "I forgive you. I have already forgiven you both. Thank you," she said, solemnly.

The truth was as Donald had said, all their pleas for

forgiveness changed nothing. She was still a lone teenage mother, without an education and without a means to support herself and her child. And truthfully, she had made choices too. And she felt partly responsible for the situation she now found herself in. She wiped her tears.

"Thank you, Chinyere," Donald and Osinachi said, as they rose to their feet. "We hope it is still okay if we adopt Fortune?"

Chinyere's heart began to race. She turned to them, feeling as though the sun was just coming out. "*Fortune?*"

Donald smiled at Osinachi. "Yes. That's the name we decided to call her... Do you like it?"

Chinyere nodded happily. "Why?"

"Because to us, she's a fortune. A gift and a blessing."

Chinyere smiled. "I mean... *Why?* She's not your child..."

"We've loved her since we knew she was coming... If no one else will claim her, we will. It doesn't matter if she isn't related by blood," Osinachi said.

Chinyere gasped and covered her mouth but couldn't hold back the sobs. "Thank you! Thank you!"

Osinachi embraced Chinyere and pulled Donald in for a group hug.

***

Osinachi and Donald left Chinyere and Fortune at the hospital for the night. They would return in the morning to conclude on the paperwork for the adoption and take their daughter home. Donald was in deep thought as they drove home. Osinachi was thanking God for all that happened today and it was making him uncomfortable.

"How can you think God had anything to do with what happened today? I don't understand why you still believe in God after what happened to Chinyere..."

"I am thanking God for all He did despite what men tried to do... I am thanking Him because He made good what was meant to destroy us... Maybe you should think about it like that."

"But why did He let Chinyere get gang raped?!"

"Are you forgetting that real men did those things...just the way you did what you did? Yet God brought salvation. He used the taxi driver who intervened," Osinachi said.

"But if the others she'd asked had just given her a lift, she wouldn't have been raped! Why do you say it was God when good people do good things, and then say it wasn't God, when bad people do bad things?"

"I don't say that. I know that sometimes, even bad things are sent by God, to purify us. My belief in God is in His *control*, in His *wisdom* and in His *goodness*. No matter what happens, good or bad, I know that God is in control. I know that He is wise and knows just why He lets things happen, even when I do not understand. And I know that He is good, and ultimately, it will all work out for our good. When it's going great, I rejoice, because it is easy and wonderful to praise Him in those times. And when things are not going well, I *trust* Him and rejoice in WHO He is, knowing that He loves me, and ultimately it will end in praise."

"So, do you think Chinyere is praising God now...?"

"If she isn't today, she will tomorrow..." Osinachi said, smiling. "Some days we cry...and those days help us appreciate the days we smile and laugh all the more. I also don't know what her relationship with God is like. If you do not know who God is, you can't have this assurance."

"How can you know it's not just in your head, though?" Donald asked, cautiously.

"Are you *really* going to go there?" Osinachi eyed him and gave a small smile. "In the world of Science, you only believe in the existence of matter. Everything must be material, and so even the mind is broken down to biology, hormones and all. But I fail to accept that we know everything, enough to conclude that if we can't see and touch it, it isn't there. If there's one thing we can learn from Science, it is that we do not know *half* of what we think we know. There are many things only belief in a God that is beyond matter and time answers. And I believe God has made Himself known to us...and to me, in a very real way. I believe in Him much more than I believe in the quality of the road we are driving on..."

"So, you're *absolutely* sure He's not an idea someone put in your head...?"

"Nothing comes from nothing..."

"Hmmm..." Donald contemplated, as they pulled into their driveway. "The end of all arguments."

THE EPILOGUE

June 2012. Princeton University, New Jersey, USA.

Good afternoon fellow graduates, administrators and teachers, friends and family. It is an honour for me to stand before you today as the Valedictorian of the Class of 2012 and commend you all for a job well done! Today is a great day, a landmark day in our pursuit for knowledge, purpose and happiness. Today, we reflect on the journey so far, we celebrate all we have been able to achieve, and also reassess and refocus our vision for the future.

First of all, I must give thanks to God. I stand here today by His amazing grace. I praise Him for all that He saw me through and the many ways He has moulded me to be the woman I am today. I give Him all the glory for all I've been able to accomplish, because I know that without Him, I can do nothing.

I also want to thank all my colleagues. You guys have been so amazing! We have been through a lot together, learnt from each other, hurt, forgiven and carried one another. I remember when we learnt that Mariam Anderson had cancer, and how everyone pulled together to raise funds for her treatment. It was a phenomenal moment for all of us when she won the battle against cancer, and today, she stands proudly with us! Amazing!

I particularly want to appreciate my best friends, Anita Hopewell and Bola Adenike. Their encouragement and belief in me have given me the confidence to persevere through many challenges, including a couple of heartbreaks. Everyone needs friends like you two! God bless Mrs Douglas and Mr. Andrews. They are two teachers whose love for their profession was infectious and seen in everything they did. I think everyone will agree with me when I say you guys are so inspiring. Thank you!

I also want to thank my parents, Mr. and Mrs Chukwuma, for giving me life, love and opportunities. I love you so much! And I can't but thank my sponsors and mentors, Mr. and Mrs Peterson, whose love and support have given me wings to fly. Who would have thought that a small village girl, turned house help in Abuja, Nigeria, would become a First Class Social Science Graduate of Criminology from the acclaimed Princeton University, in America?!

This is just to say never close the book on anyone, nor underestimate what you or anyone can be tomorrow. And never miss an opportunity to make an impact in someone else's life. Even if they never pay it back, they will pay it forward through the contributions they will make in the world. Osinachi and Donald, I will certainly pay it forward! I love you guys!

People ask me all the time why Criminology? It's not one of the things you hear children say they are interested in studying. You're likely to hear "I want to be a doctor when I grow up..." or even a policeman or woman. Actually, in my country, no one wants to be a policeman! And fewer want to be teachers! The most common answer to the question "what do you want to be when you grow up?" is probably "an accountant!" Even in my village! It seems everyone knows that's the profession where you get to count money for a living!

But seriously, I didn't think about criminology or even criminal justice, until I came face to face with the criminal justice system in my country. Until *I* became a victim, not only at the hands of civilians, but at the hands of those entrusted with the responsibility of upholding the law. I had to deal with my disagreement with the law, in the sense that the victim wasn't the primary focus in the pursuit of justice. The focus seemed more on punishing criminals than correcting wrong. I saw a failing system that didn't protect those it was created to protect, but only served those who had the power to abuse it.

I wanted to study crime to understand the mind of criminals and repeat offenders. I wanted to study legal systems that work and learn how I can influence policies and procedures in my country. I wanted to understand why laws and jails and prisons were ineffective in changing people and consider alternatives to punitive measures. I saw that the way the law was structured, it was actually impossible to enforce in its entirety, and that was also a hindering factor in getting the people to abide by the law... There is no real incentive to change, and few, if any, facilities to re-educate those who offend.

From my study of Criminology, I believe that the future lies in restorative justice. I believe what the Bible says in 1 Peter 4:8; that "*love covers a multitude of sins*". I believe in second chances. I believe there's a place for forgiveness and restoration, even in the criminal justice system. I want to be part of those who restructure our laws and legal system, so that more lives are saved from being wasted in prisons. I think if more time and resources are spent on education and rehabilitation, our communities would be safer and much more prosperous.

Why am I saying all this? Well, I know many of you will go on to be scientists, doctors, policemen and women, lawyers, accountants, social workers, teachers, artists and so much more. You've learnt a lot from your period of study here, and one of the things I know we have all learnt is the importance of questioning everything and seeking the best!

Do not be afraid to challenge the systems you enter. Do not be afraid to be the difference. All life is growth and change, and *you* are the change the world is waiting for.

I challenge you all today to keep learning. To keep questioning. To keep growing and changing. To seek the best and to be the best in all that you do!

Congratulations Class of 2012! We did it! And we will do it! God bless us all!

I am your Valedictorian, Chinyere Chukwuma.

- THE END -

Cited Reference (s):
https://en.wikipedia.org/wiki/Schizophrenia

ABOUT THE AUTHOR

Hi, my name is Ufuoma Emerhor-Ashogbon. I am a young professional, a social entrepreneur and the Founder/CEO of Fair Life Africa Foundation, a charity that supports under-privileged children. I go by the penname, Ufuomaee. I love to write and tell stories on my blog, blog.ufuomaee.org, and I also use this avenue to share about my faith in God. I am known for writing Christian romantic fiction, with lots of drama and scandal, that challenges all to think about their lifestyle and choices. I am married to Toritseju Ashogbon, a Creative Artist and a Businessman. We have a son called Jason. We live in Lagos, Nigeria.

CONNECT WITH ME

BECOME A PATRON: www.patreon.com/ufuomaee
AUTHOR PAGE: www.amazon.com/author/ufuomaee
FOLLOW ON FACEBOOK: @ufuomaeedotcom
TWITTER: @UfuomaeeB
INSTAGRAM: @ufuomaee
WEBSITE: www.ufuomaee.org
BLOG: blog.ufuomaee.org
EMAIL: me@ufuomaee.com

Check out my full catalogue of books at
books.ufuomaee.org

Printed in Poland
by Amazon Fulfillment
Poland Sp. z o.o., Wrocław